THE FIRST RULE OF FAKING IT

A. RIVERS

*To all my fellow chocolate addicts.
You can't tell me you've never
considered becoming a chocolatier.*

ONE

"Why don't you go home early and surprise your boyfriend?" Keysha suggested, carefully positioning the last truffle atop the extravagant arrangement intended to be the centerpiece of the bridal table at a wedding that weekend. "I can finish up here. The hard part is done."

"Hmm." I was reluctant to leave before the centerpiece was delivered. Coco Luxe was my business, and it was my reputation on the line if this order didn't arrive at its destination looking absolutely perfect. But Thad had been complaining about how long I spent at work, so perhaps, if I got to his place early, it would ease some of the tension that seemed to exist between us lately.

"Go on." Keysha waved her hands at me, ushering me away, her teeth bright against her dark skin as she smiled. "I've got this. I'll have it packed up and safely in the happy couple's hands before the hour is out. I'll even send photographic evidence."

I looked around the room. The counter was mostly clear,

although the sweet, rich scent of chocolate still permeated everything. The dishes had been tidied away and the materials needed to complete the commission were all on hand.

Keysha was right. There wasn't much left to do. Couple that with the fact the storefront had closed an hour ago and perhaps it really wouldn't be so bad for me to leave.

The tension dissipated from my shoulders, and they slumped. "Thanks, Key. Are you sure you'll be all right?"

"Absolutely." She snapped a tea towel toward me like a whip. "Now, get."

Laughing, I backed away. "Thanks. You're the best."

Her lips twisted smugly. "I know. Just remember that next time I'm due for a raise."

"I will."

I washed my hands, removed my apron and hung it on the hook behind the door that led through to the shop, then I grabbed my sweater and pulled it over my head. It was always a little chilly in Coco Luxe because we couldn't risk our product melting. Despite that, I tended to wear short sleeves during work hours, so I wouldn't accidentally mix any clothing fibers in the chocolate.

Calling out a farewell, I exited through the back door, making sure to lock it behind me. We weren't in a bad neighborhood, but it was always better to be safe than sorry.

I drove my small Nissan hatchback home, leaving the company vehicle for Keysha to use for the delivery. I parked in the lot and hurried into my apartment for a quick shower. Thad didn't like it when I smelled like chocolate, which was pretty much always.

I bundled my hair atop my head and scrubbed myself with my favorite lychee-scented soap, then rinsed off, dried, and changed into a pair of dark-washed jeans I had to shimmy to get into and a black button-up blouse.

I stacked a neatly folded change of clothes into my overnight bag, along with my travel toiletries, and slung it over my shoulder, then tucked my wallet into my front pocket, my phone into my back pocket, and locked the door as I departed.

The drive to Thad's apartment building didn't take long, but the contrast between the areas surrounding his place and mine was extreme. I always felt a little nervous there.

I scanned the shadowed edges of the parking garage as I made my way across it, moving as quickly as I dared in my kitten-heel boots. I pushed the elevator button and, once I was inside, relaxed a little.

I got out on his floor, walked to his door, knocked, and waited. He didn't respond. Perhaps I should have messaged before I left, so he knew to expect me.

Oh, well. I was here now.

I tried the handle, but it was locked. Glancing up and down the deserted corridor, ignoring the questionable stains on the off-white wallpaper, I debated whether to call or just let myself in.

I pressed my ear to the door. The faint whump and beep of electropop music filtered through. Perhaps he hadn't heard my knock above the music.

I pulled my phone from my back pocket, found his number, and hit Call. The phone rang out. I sighed. There was nothing for it but to go in.

I'd dumped the keys in my bag, so I dug around until I felt the pointed metal against my fingertips, then flicked through until I found the blue one that Thad had given me for his apartment. I slotted it into the lock, turned it, and tried the handle again. The door opened.

The mouthwatering aroma of sweet and sour pork greeted me. I padded into the open plan living area. Chinese take-out containers covered the kitchen counter, along with an empty beer bottle and a half-drunk glass of wine.

I frowned. Thad didn't like wine. He must have had a friend over.

The music was coming from deeper in the apartment, so I crossed the living area into the short hall. The bathroom door stood open, the room empty. The throbbing beat emanated from the bedroom.

I reached for the door, but another sound stopped me in my tracks.

My frown deepened.

Was that...?

Had that been a feminine gasp?

A long, womanly moan removed any doubt.

Dread curled in my gut. Perhaps he was just watching porn, but my mind flashed back to that wine glass, and I tried to remember whether there had been a lipstick mark on the rim.

A male grunt. Definitely Thad.

My throat tightened and my hand shook as I reached for the door and cracked it open.

The familiar sound of skin slapping against skin met my ears, and the air stank of sex.

My gut rolled over.

A dozen possible scenarios ran through my mind in which there were perfectly reasonable explanations for what my senses were telling me, but none of them seemed feasible.

Needing to know the truth, I pushed the door again, widening the crack until I could see a strip of bed.

"Fuck, baby. Let me taste those tits."

The bottom dropped out of my stomach. I reeled backward, inadvertently knocking the door open even wider with my foot.

I stared, horrified, at the sight of my boyfriend's ass clenching as he thrust into another woman.

He buried his face in the crook of her neck, revealing her face.

My *cousin's* face.

"Coral?" I choked out, unable to help myself.

Coral's eyes flew open, the shade of blue almost the exact same as mine. Her lips parted in shock, and she scrambled backward, shoving Thad away and grabbing the pillow from the other side of the bed to shield her naked body.

My back hit the wall, knocking the breath out of me.

Clearly realizing that something was wrong, Thad looked around, a scowl twisting the chiseled planes of his face as his gaze locked on me.

"You shouldn't be finished at work yet," he said, as if my being there early was the problem, not whatever the hell was going on between my boyfriend and my cousin.

Perhaps, to him, it was.

I had no way of knowing if this was a one-off thing or if he and Coral had been screwing around behind my back for weeks —or even months.

Bile rose in my throat. I grimaced as the bitter tang filled my mouth, then forced myself to swallow it back down.

"What's going on?" I demanded, though it was painfully obvious. I just wanted them to have to say it. To look me in the eye and admit what they were doing.

"Tally, I'm so sorry!" Coral slung her legs off the edge of the bed and took a step toward me.

My gaze traveled of its own accord down the long, slender length of her body. The pillow didn't hide much. Her cheeks flushed red and she snatched the sheet off the bed and wrapped it around herself.

I made myself look away from her, summoning every bit of strength I possessed to stand my ground. I wanted to wilt in the face of this betrayal—not just from my boyfriend, but from my own flesh and blood too.

It didn't help that Coral looked like a supermodel. With her slim build, flawless golden skin, and a mass of dirty-blond hair streaked with natural highlights, she could have been the poster woman for any surf brand. Never mind that we didn't live anywhere near the ocean.

Thad reclined against the remaining pillow, emotions flitting through his eyes and leaving just as swiftly. A flicker of embarrassment, followed by defiance.

He met my gaze. "Perhaps if you were more available and put more of an effort into being here for me when I need you, then I wouldn't have had to find someone else." His gaze skimmed down my body. "Losing a few pounds wouldn't have hurt either."

"Excuse me?" Outraged, I glared at him. "This isn't my fault, you asshole. Don't you dare blame your bad behavior on me."

His sheer audacity stunned me. And made me want to punch him in the face. Maybe put a kink in that long, straight nose of his.

"First of all, I know you don't like the hours I work, but if it was a deal breaker, then you should have either told me so I could decide whether to change or just ended things. Secondly, I weigh the exact same as I did when we met. You thought I was sexy then, so don't try to gaslight me about it now."

I knew I was thickly built, but I was fit from years of Pilates and yoga, and I liked my figure. Plenty of men had proven they had no problem with it either. Some had even rhapsodized over the curve of my breasts and ass.

"Fuck. You," I enunciated.

Because seriously, screw him.

A lot of plus size women I knew were self-conscious about

their weight, and if he'd pulled this same shit on them, they might have bought into it. How dare he try to play into anyone's insecurities like that?

"In case it isn't clear, we're over." I turned away from him and started for the door, but a hand landed on my arm. Small but with a firm grip. "Let me go," I growled at Coral, tears stinging the backs of my eyes. I had to get away from them before my emotions got the better of me.

"Tally, I—"

I yanked my arm away from her and ran from the bedroom, my bag jostling on my shoulder with each step. I bolted across the living area, out of the apartment, down the corridor and into the elevator, where I collapsed against the wall.

I stared back down the hall, afraid that one of them—probably Coral—might try to follow me, but no one had emerged by the time the doors hissed shut with painful slowness.

I jabbed a button and fought a wave of nausea as the elevator carried me down to the basement parking garage. The doors opened and I peered around, trying to keep my wits about me, but all I could focus on was getting to my car.

I rushed across the concrete floor, my heels clacking loudly. Thank God the keys were still safely in my grip. I pushed the key fob to unlock the car, grabbed the handle, and dove inside, pushing the button again to lock myself in.

Then, as I drew in a shaky breath, the tears finally began to stream down my face.

What the hell was I supposed to do now?

Alec.

I had to call Alec.

My best friend.

The guy who was always there for me.

He'd know what to do.

I found my phone and tried to bring up his number but was trembling too badly to hit the right buttons.

It's okay, I soothed myself. *Thad is an asshole. And Coral is a bitch. Just keep breathing. Don't let them get into your head.*

With my emotions a little more under control, I was finally able to dial Alec's number. I waited, scarcely daring to breathe, for him to pick up. When he did, the tears came even faster.

"Tally?" he asked. "What's wrong, cocobug?"

TWO

ALEC

"Thad... I... He... Ugh, I can't fucking believe..."

I shook my head, unable to make sense of Tally's mutterings. Her voice was thick and she was obviously upset. That asshole boyfriend of hers must have done something. My fists clenched at my side. There were days when I wanted nothing more than to wipe the shit-eating grin off that smug bastard's face.

Unfortunately, he seemed to have written the playbook when it came to managing my best friend.

"Hang on a sec, cocobug." I heaved my gear bag over my shoulder and shoved the changeroom door open. Hearing her was difficult enough without the kerfuffle of my teammates in the background. Once I was in the corridor, I dropped my bag to the floor and leaned against the wall. "Where are you?"

She sniffed. "In the parking garage of Thad's apartment building."

Right. As I'd expected. The jerk had fucked up.

"Are you driving?"

"N-no. I'm still parked."

"Good. Don't move. I'm coming to get you."

"Are you sure?" Her voice was small. Hesitant. "I don't want to be a nuisance."

My teeth ground together. I hated the sound of her uncertainty. I'd always been there for her in the past and always would be in the future. She should know that—no questions asked. It was his fault she had doubts.

"Yeah," I replied. "Stay right where you are. I'll be there soon."

"Okay," she whispered. "Thank you."

"No problem." I ended the call and exhaled roughly, forcing my fingers to uncurl from around the phone before I crushed it.

"Everything okay?"

I glanced up, surprised to find Seth Dexter, one of my teammates on the Colorado Dragons NHL team, standing in front of me, his brow scrunched with concern.

I sighed. "Something has upset Tally. Do you think you could have some pad thai from Siam Palace delivered to her apartment? I need to go and pick her up before she decides to drive herself home when she's clearly not in a good headspace to be behind the wheel."

"Sure." He withdrew his phone from his pocket, already opening a food delivery app. "Anything for you?"

"Whatever's easiest. I'm not fussy." I slapped his shoulder. "Thanks, man."

"No problem. Go get your girl."

I grimaced as I hefted my bag back over my shoulder and rushed toward the exit. My teammates were always calling Tally that. "My girl." Never mind the fact we'd only ever been friends. She was the most important person in my life besides my parents and sister, so to them, that made her mine.

I didn't hate it, but I always felt uncomfortable when they used that phrase around her. I didn't want her to think I was lying about our relationship status.

The parking lot of our stadium, The Lair, was nearly empty. My Jeep was right near the door, so I clicked the fob to unlock it, dumped my gear in the back, and jumped into the front within a matter of seconds.

I drove as quickly as I dared to Thad's apartment building. I couldn't risk getting pulled over for speeding but I didn't want to risk Tally getting tired of waiting for me and deciding to just drive home herself either.

Once I'd entered the complex, I circled the lot until I spotted her small, silver hatchback and pulled into a parking spot opposite. By the time I got out of my car, she'd already climbed out of hers. She threw herself into my arms and buried her face in my chest.

I caught a quick glimpse of red-rimmed eyes and tear-stained cheeks before my arms wrapped around her and I held her close.

"Shh, it's okay." I rocked her back and forth. "You're all right."

The teams we played against would laugh themselves stupid if they ever saw what a softy I was with my best friend. To the rest of the world, I was an NHL legacy with a no-nonsense game face. But I didn't have to be that guy when I was with Tally.

"What's wrong?" I asked, repeating my earlier question.

She pulled back and shook her head, her lips pressed tightly together as she tried to gather herself.

"Okay. How about I get you home and then we can talk?" What I'd really like was to march upstairs and hand Thad's ass to him for whatever he'd done to her, but that wasn't what she needed just then.

She nodded.

"Do you want anything from your car?"

"Just my bag," she rasped, her voice rough with emotion.

I opened her driver's side door, leaned in, and grabbed the bag, then I gently took the keys from her and locked the car. "Come on. I'll drive."

"But my car..."

"We can come back for it tomorrow." No way in hell was I letting her drive in the state she was in. I escorted her to my Jeep, circled to the passenger side, and helped her in. Her chin trembled as I closed the door, but she didn't break down again.

Neither of us spoke as I drove us to her apartment. We walked to her door, and I let us inside. Warm air wafted out. Tally tolerated enough cold at Coco Luxe that she liked to have the heat pump set to turn on automatically at home, so she never had to worry about returning to an icy apartment.

The lights were off, so I flicked the switch beside the door and lit up the entranceway. Tally didn't protest as I guided her to the cozy living room, with its large, cream-colored couch and matching beanbags. She dropped onto the couch and I turned on the fairy lights hanging from the curtain rail. They provided enough illumination for me to light the candle in the center of the coffee table, which smelled a little like sugar cookies.

Finally, I made my way to the kitchen, pulled a large bottle of white wine out of the minibar, which she always kept well-stocked, and poured a generous portion into a glass. I brought it to her, set it on the coffee table, and sat. She snuggled closer, and I pulled her against my side, my hand resting on the curve of her waist.

"Are you ready to tell me?" I asked quietly.

She looked down at her hands, studying them as though they were the most fascinating things she'd ever seen. "I finished work a little early and went over to surprise Thad. He was surprised all right. He was fucking Coral when I walked in."

Rage burned through my veins like lava. "He was what?"

Fury rose in the back of my throat, and my hands twitched. I shouldn't have held back. I should have gone up to Thad's apartment and crushed the smarmy shit.

She shrugged, as if it was nothing, but I knew her and could tell it was all an act. This had hurt her. Deeply. "He cheated on me."

"With your cousin." How goddamned despicable.

I'd never liked Thad. He wasn't right for Tally. I mean, come on, the guy disliked chocolate. There was something fundamentally wrong with him. But I'd never thought he'd cheat on her. Who the hell would? Tally was beautiful, talented, and successful. Any man would have to be an idiot to throw her away.

"Then he's the dumbest fuck I've ever met," I said bluntly.

As for Coral, she definitely wasn't the person I'd thought she was either. I'd always known that Tally's cousin was a bit self-centered—Coral's sister and mother were too—but this went beyond selfishness. It was downright cruel.

"Stay here." I disentangled myself from her, went to her bedroom, and collected her favorite pair of cozy pajamas from her bed, along with a fluffy blanket. I grabbed the softest pair of socks from her drawer and carried the bundle out, presenting it to her. "Change into this. You'll feel better."

It was one of the things I'd learned about her during our years of friendship. Nothing soothed her like warm, comfortable clothes, food, and wine. Throw in a romantic period drama and her tears would be gone in no time.

Hopefully.

Thad-the-asshole certainly wasn't worth them.

I backed out of the room and lingered in the hall, giving her plenty of time to change. When I reentered, she was tucked up on the sofa with the blanket wrapped around her and her fluffy feet poking out from beneath her.

The doorbell rang. Her eyes widened.

"That will be the food," I explained, so she wouldn't worry about having to face anyone while she was in this state.

I answered the door and accepted the delivery, making sure to keep my chin down in case the delivery guy happened to be an ice hockey fan. As soon as he was gone, I took the take-out to the kitchen and served the pad thai on one plate and emptied the other container—what looked to be khao man gai chicken rice—onto the other.

Carrying both plates to the coffee table, along with two sets of cutlery, I noticed her watching me, her eyes hooded in the dimly lit space. The light from the candle danced across the silverware as I placed it before her and sat.

She bit her lower lip. "I don't feel like eating."

"Just give it a try," I urged.

Tally was the kind of person who needed regular meals or she got hangry, which wouldn't help our current situation.

Reluctantly, she straightened, her feet dropping to the floor as she leaned forward and grabbed the cutlery. She pierced a piece of mushroom and popped it into her mouth, chewing slowly, then twirled noodles around her fork. Relieved to see she was eating, I dug into my own meal. I'd probably need something else later, but this would tide me over for now.

"He's going to regret losing you," I promised when I'd made it halfway through the khao man gai. "You're way too good for him, and he knows it."

At least, if he had more than two brain cells, he would.

She didn't look convinced.

"It's true," I insisted. "You have so much going for you. You're pretty, you own a business, you're smart and ambitious and a magician in the kitchen. He's an overgrown man child who was too stupid to see how good he had it."

Her lips twisted and she glanced away.

"What is it?" I asked, my gut clenching. I didn't like her expression. It made me want to drive back to Thad's apartment and kick him in the balls while wearing my skates.

"Nothing," she muttered. "Just something he said. I know better than to take it seriously."

"What did he say?" And how badly did I need to make him regret it?

She twisted her hands on her lap. "He implied that I work too much, and that I need to lose weight."

"Fuck that noise." I set my fork down, so disgusted I wasn't sure I could finish the chicken. "You should live your goddamn best life, and if that means focusing on the kickass business that you've created all by yourself, then there's absolutely nothing wrong with that."

"I know." She picked some more at her pad thai. "But it's hard to remember sometimes."

"Then consider this your reminder. And," I added, meeting her eyes and holding her gaze until I knew she was listening properly, "you are gorgeous."

Her cheeks colored and she dipped her chin, unable to hold my gaze for any longer. "You're biased."

"But my teammates aren't. Several of them have said how hot they think you are." If I hadn't warned them off, at least a couple would have hit on her. But they weren't long-term relationship guys, and she deserved more than a one-night stand, so I'd made sure they knew not to lay a finger on her.

She shrugged, obviously dubious. I decided to try a different tactic.

"Want me to put on Pride and Prejudice?" I asked.

The slightest grin hooked the corner of her mouth. "The BBC version?"

"As if you have to ask." I knew that the BBC version was her favorite.

I started streaming the show and kept an eye on her as I finished my meal. She ate enough pad thai for me not to worry, but her appetite wasn't what it usually was. I'd have to check in on her regularly to make sure she was doing all right.

She snuggled up against my side, and I made room for her to rest her head against my shoulder as she watched people in historical dresses dance on TV.

A while later, she dozed off. I stayed where I was despite the rumbling of my gut demanding more food. I'd have to move at some point, but for now, I didn't want to disturb her.

Her phone rang, and I snatched it up before it woke her and checked the Caller ID. Then, scowling, I rejected the call and blocked Coral's number. She should know better than to bother Tally after what she'd put her through.

For good measure, I went into the contacts and blocked Thad's number too. Tally wouldn't approve, but what she didn't know couldn't hurt her.

THREE

TALLY

"Won't be at work today," I murmured as I typed the message out to Keysha and sent it, then collapsed against my pillow and closed my eyes, hoping she wouldn't ask why. I felt bad for calling in sick, especially after leaving early last night, but I just couldn't face the shop.

All of those people, so bustling and happy, expecting me to be cheerful too. Usually, I managed just fine, but my heart and ego were both a little bruised. Not to mention the fact my eyes were puffy and probably red. I hadn't looked in a mirror yet, so I could live in blissful ignorance for a while longer.

At least the day should be quiet at Coco Luxe, so Keysha wouldn't have to deal with much beyond walk-in customers. We had no outstanding commissions. I'd already seen her message from last night about how pleased the bride and groom were with their centerpiece. It had almost made me smile.

My phone buzzed.

Keysha: *Are you okay? Do you need anything?*

I groaned. She was too good to me. I owed her the truth.

I probably would too. But I needed a little more time to get myself together first, and that meant coffee.

With a grunt of effort, I tossed the covers back and swung my feet off the bed. They hit the floor, and I gave myself a moment to adjust before standing. I wandered through the apartment to the kitchen, phone in hand.

I had a good quality coffee maker, which I started up, and meanwhile, scanned the room for any mess remaining from last night. There wasn't anything. Alec must have tidied up before he left. God bless the man. I wondered whether he'd gone home last night or if he'd slept on the couch before driving in for practice bright and early.

Hopefully, the former. The couch wasn't built for a man his size to use as a bed.

I scanned the fridge, trying to recall whether I might have left anything good inside, and spotted the creamy cardboard wedding invitation held to the door by a magnet. The elegant gold calligraphy stared at me accusingly.

My lower lip wobbled.

Damn, I'd forgotten about my cousin Lake's wedding next month. Lake was Coral's older sister, and Thad and I had already RSVP'd to attend her destination wedding in Hawaii together.

Now, I'd have to go alone.

Not only that, but I was confronted by the very real possibility that all my extended family may know—or hear sometime between now and then—what had been going on between Coral and Thad behind my back. I'd have to face their pity or judgment.

It would be humiliating.

My throat tightened and my eyes prickled, but I was all out of tears. That was something, at least.

The machine beeped and I served myself a mug of coffee and drained it in seconds. I refilled and placed the mug on the kitchen counter while I tapped out a message to Lake. If I was going to have to embarrass myself, I might as well get the first step over with while I was already wallowing.

Tally: *Thad won't be accompanying me to your wedding anymore. Sorry for any inconvenience.*

There. That sounded polite. Professional. There was no silent accusation about whether she might have known that her younger sister was screwing my boyfriend.

I took my coffee to the couch and set it down while I lit the vanilla-scented candle in the center of the coffee table.

Lake: *I know. Coral called last night and said he'd be coming with her. Sorry if it's awkward for you, but chin up. There are plenty of fish in the sea.*

My jaw dropped. What. The. Hell?

It had never occurred to me that Coral, the man-stealer, might blatantly bring my ex as her date to her sister's wedding. There would be no hiding the situation either. Coral was a bridesmaid, which meant people would pay attention both to her and her partner.

I buried my face in my hands to muffle my scream.

I should pull out. Just not go.

That would be the best thing to do. Then I wouldn't have to see Thad and Coral playing at being a happy couple and no one would be whispering about my failed relationship behind my back.

But I already had the plane tickets. I'd booked a non-refundable room at the resort where the wedding was being held. Was I really willing to give up a week in Hawaii because of those two awful human beings?

It might be worth it. The humiliation factor would be huge. But still. I'd never been to Hawaii before, and if I didn't go now, then it would look like I was ashamed and hiding away. Perhaps the hiding part was accurate, but I had nothing to be ashamed of.

They were the ones who ought to be ashamed.

I wrapped my hands around my cup of coffee and drank deeply, hoping the caffeine would make the right course of action more clear. Unfortunately, all it did was make me aware enough to realize I hadn't brushed my teeth last night and no doubt had terrible morning breath. I undoubtedly also could use an all-round freshen up.

I considered leaving the rest of the coffee but decided the extra kick might be nice, so I finished the mug and headed for the shower.

Once I'd been scrubbed from top to bottom and my mouth was minty fresh, I dressed in jeans and a top and debated how to fill the day. I could just flop on the couch and finish watching Pride and Prejudice, but I'd done enough wallowing last night. I needed to keep myself at least slightly busy.

Perhaps I should make something for Alec to show how much I appreciate him? He'd been my rock last night, coming to pick me up, getting me Thai food, coddling me and reminding me that at least one person always had my back.

Yeah, Alec deserved a treat.

I racked my brain. It would have to be something that wouldn't interfere with his NHL-player, high protein, low-junk-food diet. There was a tasty dark chocolate nut praline that he liked. Perhaps I'd make that.

I strode to the kitchen and checked the cupboards. I had enough ingredients to whip something together. I weighed out the correct portion of dark chocolate and was about to start melting it as part of the tempering process when my phone rang.

I stiffened and my gut clenched. What if it was Thad? Or Coral? Or, god forbid, Lake following up on her message about the wedding. I couldn't handle speaking to any of them. Checking the screen, my shoulders relaxed when I saw that it was only Mom. I answered and put it on speaker phone.

"Hey, darling. How are you?" she asked, a hint of caution in her usually cheerful tone.

I narrowed my eyes. "Okay."

"Are you really?" she persisted. "It's just that Alec said you might want to talk to me about something."

I sighed. Of course he had. While he was my rock, Alec wasn't exactly the most emotionally expressive person in the world, so whenever he was worried he might have fallen short in that regard, he brought in my mother as his reinforcement. She was all about talking things out and letting ourselves feel what we feel.

"Thad and I broke up last night."

"Oh, baby. I'm sorry to hear that."

I raised my eyebrows, unconvinced. She may be relentlessly cheerful, but I always had the feeling she saw something in Thad that I didn't, which made her wary of him. Perhaps I should have paid more attention to her instincts.

"I walked in on him with another woman." To my relief, my voice didn't break.

She gasped. "Who? Was it someone you knew? What were they doing?"

I hesitated. What was I supposed to say? He was balls-deep in your niece?

"Let's just say that my timing was really, really bad, and that there were no clothes, and the person with him was, uh, Coral."

"As in, sweet cousin Coral?"

"Yes," I ground out. "In all her naked glory."

"Oh." She was quiet for a moment. "I'm sorry, darling. That must have been horrible for you. I'm not sure what came over your cousin, but I hope she's ashamed of herself. As for that Thad... Well, let's just say that you're better off without him."

"I am," I agreed, more forcefully than necessary. "Good riddance." Unfortunately, the last two words squeaked out, betraying my upset.

Mom made a sympathetic sound. "Please tell me you didn't leave anything at his place?"

"Nope." Other than my car, which I'd have to sort out later. I'd never felt comfortable leaving a change of clothes in one of his drawers or my toiletries in his bathroom. Maybe my subconscious knew he couldn't be trusted.

"At least you won't ever have to see him again then."

I opened my mouth to tell her about the wedding but then closed it. I still wasn't sure if I'd even go, and if I told Mom that Thad was attending with Coral, she'd have words with her sister, and the whole thing would spiral. Best to leave it alone for now.

We talked for a while longer, and then I got busy making the dark chocolate praline for Alec.

Late in the afternoon, there was a firm knock on the door. I checked through the peephole to confirm it was Alec and let him in.

"I have something for you," I said, waving him through the living area toward the kitchen.

He put his hand on my shoulder to stop me before I pulled away. I froze. The familiar citrusy scent of his soap tickled my nostrils, along with the natural aroma of clean man, and I did my best to stop breathing.

Fresh from his post-training shower, he always smelled so sexy. It had been years since my libido first noticed that Alec was hot as hell in addition to being gruff and kind and thoughtful, but I could usually compartmentalize my reaction to him.

Unfortunately, today my defenses were down.

"You doing okay?" he asked, his touch scalding me even through my shirt. His eyes, that familiar shade of brown, searched my own, and I forced myself not to notice the ropy muscles of his tattooed forearm or the breadth of his powerful shoulders.

Just a friend, I reminded myself. *Get it together.*

"I've been better, but I could be worse." I backed off and led him to the kitchen, where the dark chocolate pralines were arranged on the counter. "For you. They need a little while longer to set properly. I'll put them in a box when you leave so you can take them with you."

Alec flashed me a rare grin and popped one into his mouth, closing his eyes and moaning his appreciation. My libido perked up.

Down, girl.

"I brought your car back," he said, opening his eyes again.

"How'd you manage that?"

"I grabbed the key while I was here last night and my teammates helped."

"Oh." I wasn't sure how to feel about that. I didn't want them knowing what had happened, but I did appreciate their assistance. "Make sure to thank them for me."

"I will. Did your mom call?"

"She did."

"Did talking to her help?"

"Maybe a little." Unfortunately, a conversation with my mother couldn't turn back time and cure the underlying problem, so there was only so much that talking about it could solve.

I glanced at the wedding invitation on the door, remembering her words about not seeing Thad again.

Alec followed my gaze. "Oh, shit. You'll have to see Coral at the wedding, won't you?"

I drew in a deep breath and let it out all at once. "Thad too. Apparently, she's taking him as her date."

"What the fuck?" he growled.

His reaction made me feel a little better. Like it wasn't unreasonable to be pissed off at them.

Okay, so perhaps Coral and Thad were dating now, but even so, it seemed a little cruel to take him somewhere she knew I'd be.

"I'm thinking about pulling out," I admitted.

His dark brows knitted together. "That's not right. You shouldn't have to miss out on your beach vacation because of them. You haven't done anything wrong."

I shrugged and leaned against the counter. "It's just easiest."

Anger flashed in his eyes. "Fuck that. I know you've been looking forward to it. How's this? I'll come with you. It's my bye week. That way, you don't have to deal with them on your own."

"Don't be silly. I know you mean well, but if I take my friend as my date, it will only make me look more pathetic, as if I'm not strong enough to face them on my own."

He gazed at me levelly and my cheeks heated as I recalled

that I had, essentially, just admitted that I couldn't bear the thought of dealing with them alone. Still, it was one thing to confess the truth to him. It was another entirely for Thad and Coral to know that.

He ran one of his massive hands over his buzz cut. "Then we'll say we're in love."

I snorted.

"What?" he demanded. "Everyone knows we're close. It's not that big of a leap, is it?"

"It's precisely because we've been friends for so long that it wouldn't be believable," I protested, anxiety knotting my insides at just the thought of how we might be ridiculed. "No one would believe that we suddenly woke up one day and decided to date after being strictly platonic friends for over a decade."

"Friends try dating all the time." The stubborn set of his chin indicated that he didn't intend to cede the point.

"But not us."

Maybe his argument had some merit. It wasn't unheard of for friends to get together, but I couldn't handle pretending. Not on top of everything else. I doubted we'd fool anyone, and there was a good possibility that putting on an act like that would trick my heart into believing something real could happen between us.

I was already vulnerable, and if I let myself get closer to Alec, it would only hurt more when it ended.

Alec softened. "Promise you'll think about it."

"Okay."

But I wouldn't change my mind.

Right now, my heart was bruised. If I allowed myself to believe in a fairy tale where Alec loved me, it could end up broken.

FOUR

ALEC

I skated onto the ice, scanning the seats behind the penalty box, where Tally and my family usually sat during home games. Sure enough, Tally was two rows back from the penalty box, wearing a Colorado Dragons jacket with Wright, my last name, printed on the bottom.

My heart lifted. Damn, she looked good. Her pale cheeks were flushed from the cold, her bright eyes sparkled down at me, and her rich brown hair flowed like satin around her shoulders.

Thad was an idiot.

He'd given her up, and for what?

A little attention? Some no-strings sex?

"Making heart eyes at your girl?" Gallagher asked, skating around me and coming to a stop in front of me. "Did she give you a kiss for luck?"

I smirked. "Wouldn't you like to know."

If another of the team members had asked, I'd have reminded them that Tally wasn't actually my girl, but correcting Gallagher would be like kicking a puppy. Besides, I didn't mind people thinking she was mine. Maybe it would even aid my case when I revisited my suggestion about pretending to date.

Behind Gallagher, Mom blew me a kiss and Dad mimed taking a shot at goal and made some dramatic facial expressions. I laughed. It was only his NHL legend status that prevented him from being that embarrassing goofy Dad with the bad jokes. Not that I'd mind if he was.

Cromwell, the center who'd recently transferred, skated up and gestured for me to join him for drills with the other wing. We passed the puck back and forth for a while, practicing different combinations of passes before taking shots on goal. Our goalie, Davi, blocked almost every one with unerring accuracy.

"Do you want to actually challenge me sometime today?" he called, spurring us on.

I passed to Cromwell, headed for the corner of the goal, and when he slung it back, I tapped it in.

"About time," Davi said, slapping me on the shoulder hard enough that I nearly tripped. "Do it again."

By the time the game started, I was thoroughly warmed up. Cromwell won the puck in the puck drop, and he and I raced up the ice. Just as Cromwell made to pass to me, someone blasted into me from the side, slamming me against the boards.

I shoved them off, but it was too late. The opportunity had been lost.

The other team's defense took the puck from Cromwell and sent it flying up the ice to their left wing, who tried to get it past Davi, but the puck bounced off his pads.

I skated back, keeping an eye on the situation in case I needed to move fast.

Play moved back and forth. They slipped a goal past Davi

minutes before the end of the first period and then repeated the act in the second.

Going into the third period, the Dragons were fired up. Coach wasn't happy, and unless we wanted to be skating shuttles up and down the ice for hours at practice, we'd better get our acts together.

Cromwell got the puck and passed it back to Dexter in defense. I motioned to Dexter and he skated one way then drilled it across to me. None of the defenders were close, so I made it almost all the way to the goal before they intercepted me. I flicked the puck up at the last second and it hit the back of the net.

As my teammates gathered around me, cheering, I glanced up into the stands, instinctively searching for Tally. She was bouncing up and down on the balls of her feet, clapping wildly. As she met my eyes, she cupped her hands around her mouth and hollered her support so loudly that I could hear it above everyone else.

Play resumed, but now that we'd tasted success, there was no stopping us. The frontline glided straight through the opposition's attackers, stealing the puck and taking it straight to the goal. This time, it was Cromwell who scored. I didn't care who had the honor, as long as it was us and not the opposition.

The other team fought hard for the rest of the period, no doubt knowing that the outcome of the game depended on it. It was messy. Sticks flying, bodies colliding, and more than a few drops of blood spilling on the ice. But then, minutes from the final buzzer, Gallagher passed the puck up to me, I flicked it over to the other wing, and he slipped it over the line.

We won.

The team came together, exchanging boisterous hugs and back slaps. I skated a victory lap, dragging Cromwell with me, then skated over to the barrier nearest to Tally and my family. I pressed my palm against the plastic and grinned up at them.

My heart swelled. I was so happy to have supportive parents and the world's best best-friend, who would always make the effort to be there for me and show how much they cared.

I tapped my chest and pointed to them. I may not be the best at showing emotion, courtesy of growing up in the public eye and always needing to keep a lid on things, but I never wanted them to forget or doubt how much I appreciated them.

"That's my boy!" Mom yelled.

"You killed it out there," Dad said, giving me an emphatic two thumbs up.

I snorted. Dork.

I rejoined the team, and we lined up to exchange handshakes with the opposition. As we made our way along the line, I nodded and smiled at everyone who looked friendly and tried to ignore the ones who scowled. Of course they were upset. They'd lost.

With that over, we got off the ice and headed to the changerooms. While we began to strip off, Coach Alan stood at the head of the room, notebook in hand, expression giving nothing away.

"Well, boys, you sure made me sweat that time," he said, the faintest curl of his lip indicating that he might be less than impressed by our earlier performance.

"Sorry, coach," someone called from deeper in the changeroom.

"At least you brought it around at the end," he said, then glanced down at his notebook. "I think we can agree that while we may have won tonight, there is plenty to work on. Here are a few things I noticed."

After the debrief, I showered and changed into a suit. Coach Alan had pulled Cromwell aside to speak to the media, which meant that I didn't have to, but we still had to look our best for any opportunistic photographers who might be hanging around.

I said my goodbyes and made a beeline for the door. Some of the team liked to gather for "bonding" activities after the games—i.e. getting drunk and trying to find a puck chaser to take home. I never took part in that, and they all knew as much. Especially after home games. After those, I liked to eat with my parents and talk shop.

As soon as I exited the changeroom, I spotted Tally waiting in the corridor. She straightened from where she'd been leaning against the wall, and hugged me, maneuvering around my gear bag.

"Your parents have gone to your place already," she said as she let me go. "Your mom wanted to get started on dinner."

"Any idea what she's planning for tonight?" I asked. Mom was a fantastic cook. Dad liked to play sous chef, although he'd have no idea what to do if not for her.

"I don't know, sorry," she said.

"Whatever it is, I'm sure it will be delicious." My gaze dropped to the hem of her shirt, above which my name stood out in stark white lettering. "My jacket suits you."

She blushed, and I wondered what it meant. I'd never commented on her wearing my jacket before, except to be grateful for the support, but now, considering the situation with Thad and Coral and Lake's wedding, it occurred to me again that all of those years of having her cheer on the sidelines, wearing my name for all to see, would play well into the ruse I'd suggested.

"Perhaps..." I trailed off, trying to figure out how I could word this so she wouldn't immediately say no. "Because you look so good in my jacket, and you already wear it anyway, you ought to just let me play the role of doting boyfriend. We're pretty much doing everything a couple would do."

The pink of her cheeks deepened, and my breathing stuttered.

"Well," I amended, "everything except, you know, the sex."

She giggled and clapped her hand to her mouth. "The sex?" she asked, her eyes dancing with amusement. "Did you seriously just call it 'the sex'?"

I rolled my eyes. "You know what I mean."

Her giggles faded. "It really isn't necessary. I'll be fine."

"I disagree. It's completely necessary. No one is going to get away with cheating on you and breaking your heart and then adding insult to injury by flaunting their new relationship in front of you and your entire extended family."

She pursed her lips and looked around as if checking that no one could overhear us. A few more of my team members had trailed out of the changeroom but none of them even glanced our way.

"Taking you with me and making a show of being together would only draw more attention to everything that happened." She looked down at her hands, and picked at the end of one of her short, tidy nails. "I don't want to make a big scene. All I want is to avoid humiliation."

"And you will." I put my hand on her shoulder. "You did nothing wrong. I won't let them make you feel ashamed for no reason. Take me with you. Make that asshole Thad squirm. He deserves it. I hope he's embarrassed. He should be. Let me make him regret ever hurting you."

Honestly, what I really wanted to do was punch the bastard in the face. But my agent might've had something to say about that. Mom and Dad too.

"Say yes, Tally."

She was softening, I could tell. Finally, she relented. "You'd better not make me regret it."

FIVE

TALLY

"Are you sure this is necessary?" I asked as we entered the high-end department store. The space was bright and airy, designed in a minimalist style with white floors, white walls, and high above us, a white ceiling. There were no smells, and while it wasn't cold, it certainly wasn't what I'd consider warm either. A similar temperature to the inside of Coco Luxe.

"Yes," he said simply.

"Surely, one of the suits you use for games would be fine for the wedding." I didn't want him spending heaps of money on a suit when he'd already dropped enough on a flight to join me in Hawaii.

"I need something with an X factor," he said, leading me farther into the store. "Something that will make Thad look twice, so we can really rub it in that we're there together. We want him to know that you're not pining over him, that you've got someone better and he can just go to hell."

I appreciated his willingness to put in the effort, but I really didn't think the situation called for a brand-new suit. Especially not a designer suit like the ones in the menswear section ahead of us. It was strange that he'd insisted on shopping. Alec was not the kind of guy who liked browsing the stores—especially if he could browse online instead.

Yet, for some reason, there we were.

An assistant approached us. She was dressed neatly but not so as to stand out, all smooth lines and dark colors with pale blond hair twisted into an elegant knot on the back of her head.

"How can I help you?" she asked, smiling first at me and then at Alec.

"I need a suit," Alec said gruffly.

She folded her hands one over the top of the other in front of her. "What's the occasion?"

"We're going to a wedding." He glanced at me, his dark eyes warm. "Tally's ex is going to be there. We need him to know that she's moved on to someone better."

The sales assistant grinned. "Do you want simple and elegant or flashy and eye-catching?"

Alec considered this briefly. "Something simple but with an edge."

"All right, let me find some options. You two can go and wait by the changerooms." She scanned him up and down, obviously sizing him to the best of her ability, and then pivoted and marched to one of the nearby racks.

Alec nodded toward the changeroom and we made our way over there. I sat on the crisp white sofa beside the door, which definitely wasn't designed for comfort. Still, it was better than standing.

When the sales assistant joined us, she held an assortment of suit jackets and trousers, along with shirts, ties—and was that a bowtie?

She selected a pair of trousers and a jacket and a shirt and passed them to him. "Try these first."

He took them and disappeared into the small room. The lock snicked into place. While we waited, the sales assistant organized her findings on a clothing rail nearby, presumably sorting them into the order in which she wanted him to try them on. The lock clicked, the door opened, and Alec stepped out.

My jaw dropped. My best friend always looked good. He was a good-looking man. But in the navy pinstriped suit that clung to his muscular body, he didn't just look good, he looked amazing.

"What do you think?" he asked, running his hands down the fabric of the jacket.

"Incredible," I told him.

"Agreed," the sales assistant said. "But I think we can do better."

Better? I wasn't sure I could survive "better."

For the next fifteen minutes, Alec modeled suit after suit. Some were formal, some were playful, and some were downright sexy. In the end, we opted for a suit in a gorgeous shade of blue that reminded me of a tropical beach. I thought it was fitting for the occasion.

While Alec changed back into his original outfit, the sales assistant turned to me and smiled. "You're a lucky woman. That is one delicious man."

"Oh." I blinked at her, surprised by her assumption that we were together, although perhaps I shouldn't have been considering the way Alec had phrased his request at the start. "He's not actually mine."

Scoffing, she arched an eyebrow. "Uh-huh. I see how he looks at you."

How?

How did he look at me?

We were just friends. Friends didn't look at each other any particular way. She must be imagining it.

My stomach fluttered.

But what if she isn't? What if he finds you as attractive as you find him?

Yeah, right. There was no point in wasting time or hope on silly fantasies.

Alec came out and I turned toward the counter, but before I could take a step, he said, "Do you have a dress for the wedding yet?"

I shrugged. "I've got plenty in my closet to choose from."

He shifted from one foot to the other, glancing at the sales assistant and then back at me. "You should have something new to wear. Something beautiful. I don't want you to have any reason to feel self-conscious. Let me buy it for you."

Suddenly, understanding dawned. Now I knew why he'd insisted on this uncharacteristic shopping trip. It had never been to get him a suit, although that was a bonus; the real motivation had been to find a dress for me.

"Alec..." I drew out his name, holding his gaze with a warning in my eyes. "That's sweet, but there really is no need for it."

I couldn't afford to buy a dress from here, and between the plane tickets and this suit, he was already out of pocket enough because of this wedding. I wasn't going to add to his expenses.

"You should at least look." He jerked his head toward the elevator that led up to the women's wear department. "There's no harm in that, right?"

I narrowed my eyes at him. I knew how he worked. If I let on that I saw anything I liked, he'd purchase it within two seconds flat. "No, Alec."

"Please, cocobug." He moved closer and took my hand.

"Let me do this for you. You know I have the money. I won't even notice it's been spent."

I hesitated, knowing that was true. Not only had Alec's father set up a healthy trust fund for him when he was young, but he himself earned several million dollars a year. A few thousand was nothing to him.

But it was something to me. I didn't want to take advantage of my friend.

"Come on," he cajoled, obviously sensing the fact I was weakening. "If you won't do it for you then do it for me. I want to watch Thad swallow his tongue. I want him to see what a catch you are and know he's lost you forever."

The assistant's eyes lit up, clearly spotting the potential for a big sale. "Aww, isn't that so sweet?"

Alec turned to her. "Would you be able to find some dresses for me please? Or steer me to someone who can? I think something in a shade of blue, green, pink, or purple would be best. Perhaps blue, because that would go well with her eyes?"

"Absolutely!" The saleswoman patted the suit that was laid out over her arm. "Usually, there would be someone else in that department better suited to helping you, but since we've already got your friend's suit sorted, I'd like to stick with you and see it through. I'll just put this on the counter and then I'll take you up and we can look at some dresses."

She hurried away, perhaps worried that I'd protest if she gave me the opportunity.

"Just try them on." Alec bumped my shoulder affectionately. "It won't hurt."

I sighed. "Fine."

The sales assistant returned and led us up the elevator and into a department occupied by a dazzling array of dresses in different colors, made from different fabrics, some of them long and elegant, others short and flirty.

"Do you want a similar style to the suit?" she asked. "Stylish, but not 100% formal?"

"Anything that will pair well with my suit and show off just how gorgeous Tally is," Alec replied before I was able.

My breath caught. How was I supposed to remind myself that all of this was fake when he kept calling me beautiful?

The sales assistant collected several dresses for me to try and sent me in first with a long, rich purple dress. It fit well but was cut a little lower than I'd like. Alec nodded, but she shook her head.

I tried on another, and then another, and on and on until I felt like a girl in one of those makeover montage scenes from a romantic comedy film. I couldn't deny that they made me feel good. Particularly, a pale blue one the color of shallow ocean in the tropics and a pink gown that complemented my complexion well.

I was wearing the blue dress when Alec announced, "I think you need accessories too."

The sales assistant snapped her fingers. "You're right. What do you think? A purse? Shoes? Sunglasses?"

"Everything."

She breezed away.

"No." I put my hands on my hips. "I haven't even said I'll buy one of the dresses yet."

"Because you won't." Alec smirked. "I will."

I threw my hands up in the air. "You can't just throw away your money on me."

His expression grew serious. "I don't consider this to be throwing it away. Any money spent on you is worth it."

My heart skipped. I tried to tell myself he didn't mean anything by it, but my subconscious began weaving more daydreams in which my best friend suddenly fell madly in love with me.

When the assistant returned, she was accompanied by a young, pretty Asian man who was carrying a small bench upon which sat a number of pairs of shoes. The woman held a box and from where I stood, I could see several purses within.

"That dress is perfect for you," the man said, placing the bench on the ground and doing an exaggerated chef's kiss. "May I suggest these shoes to go with it?"

I took the pair of white strappy sandals from him and turned to the woman. "What else am I matching with this?"

She offered me a white leather purse and a sunglasses case.

Half an hour later, I had two full outfits to choose from, accessorized not only with shoes, purses, and sunglasses, but also with a simple silver pendant necklace.

We'd also gathered quite an audience. Apparently, word had spread about my predicament with the wedding and my ex, and now the sales staff were personally invested in making sure I looked my absolute best.

"You know, I really don't need all this," I said to Alec, trying to keep my voice low so the observers wouldn't all hear.

"Maybe not," he murmured back. "But you deserve it. You've been my best friend for years. You've been there for every one of my important milestones. Let me do this. Nothing is too good for you."

I melted right then. Who wouldn't?

"Which dress is your favorite?" he asked.

I dithered, not really sure. Personally, I like the pink best, but I had a feeling the blue looked better, and wasn't that the point of all this?

"The blue one," I replied firmly.

"Okay then." He slung his arm around me and gave me a hug. "That wasn't so hard, was it?"

I just looked at him.

He laughed. "Think of it this way: If you were my girl, it

would be my job to spoil you. For all intents and purposes, you are my girl right now, and there's no woman I'd rather spoil than you."

"Why are you single?" I asked, baffled as always by the state of his social life. He had so much to offer. One day, someone was going to be smart enough to lock him down, and then there would be no more of these wonderful days spent together, just me and him. No girlfriend would tolerate our closeness. At least, I doubted they would.

My boyfriends had never loved our relationship, but I'd always made it clear that if they made me choose, they wouldn't win.

The sales assistants clapped as Alec announced the winning outfit. Most of them cleared away. The man from the shoes department winked over his shoulder as he left. Alec didn't let me come to the counter as the sale was put through. I guessed he didn't want me to hear exactly what the cost was, even though I had a reasonable idea anyway.

He lingered over there for longer than necessary. As I watched him, my gaze trailed to the familiar outline of his strong arms and narrow waist and I wondered what his parents would make of all of this.

I loved Mr. and Mrs. Wright. They were so kind and fun to be around. Would they take it in stride when they learned about our act, or would they be upset by us misleading people?

Not to mention my own parents. How would they react?

Alec looked over at me and whatever he saw in my expression made him frown.

"What's wrong?" he asked as he approached, carrying our purchases.

"I hope neither of our parents will be mad at us."

"Why would they be mad?"

I walked slowly as I gathered my thoughts. "It's not exactly honest, is it?"

He studied me, taking my misgivings seriously. "If you're really worried, then come over for dinner after our next game. We can talk to my parents then, and once yours realize that Thad is at the wedding, I can't see them having any issue with us pretending a little."

"Okay." I let out a shaky breath. That wasn't a bad idea. It was tradition to share dinner with his parents after his home games. We used to go to their place, but Alec often got tired early on evenings after he played so they'd taken to coming to his house instead so he didn't have to drive while tired.

Please let him be right.

SIX

ALEC

"Oops, I left my phone in my car." Tally excused herself from my kitchen, shooting a meaningful look at me on her way out.

I grimaced, knowing this was when I was supposed to break the news to my parents—who were serving steak and vegetables onto plates on the kitchen counter—that she and I were going to pretend to be dating to save her pride at Lake's wedding.

After our initial conversation, we'd gone back and forth about whether we really needed to say anything about it, but considering my high profile existence, there was every chance that a photo of us looking like a couple would make its way into the tabloids and I didn't want them to be caught off guard if it did.

I breathed in the delicious aroma of a well-cooked meal and steeled myself.

"The thing is," I began, looking down at my hands to avoid Mom's curious gaze, "Tally and I have... I mean, we're..."

Why was this so hard?

I hadn't expected it to be. It was a simple situation. I'd offered—almost insisted—on helping her, and I'd made a point of letting her know that Mom and Dad wouldn't be bothered by it, which was true. They'd probably even be proud of me for looking out for her, but for some reason, the words were sticking in the back of my throat.

"We're going to—"

At that moment, Tally reentered the room.

Damn. She hadn't been gone long enough for me to get it all out.

Tally raised an eyebrow at me. Mom caught the expression and glanced from me to her and back. Her eyes widened.

"Oh, my God, it's finally happened." She giggled gleefully. "You're dating. This is so exciting. I'm happy for you both."

"We always knew you'd make a perfect couple," Dad chimed in, his face relaxing into a smile. "You took your time about it though."

I stared at them both, wondering what the hell was going on. They thought we made a good couple?

"Y-you don't understand," Tally stammered, the whites of her eyes showing as Mom flew across the room and swept her into a hug. "We're not—"

"You don't have to hide anything from us, darling," Mom assured her, squeezing her tightly. "We're thrilled. Just thrilled."

Tally glared at me over her shoulder, her eyes spearing me like a sword. "Fix this," she mouthed.

I shrugged helplessly. They seemed so happy. I couldn't bear to disappoint them by saying it was only fake.

"How did it happen?" Dad asked, sliding the last steak onto a plate and circling around the counter to close the distance between us.

"It isn't how it—"

"It was after Tally's breakup," I blurted out, cutting her off.

Mom cocked her head. "That's right. You were seeing that finance guy. What was his name? Chad? Brad?"

"Thad," Tally corrected stiffly. I could feel her glare burning into my forehead.

"Right, right. What happened with him?"

I hadn't told them any details because Tally was embarrassed, and even though she had no reason to be, I didn't want to spread gossip that might make her uncomfortable.

Tally's upper lip curled. "He turned out to be a cheating asshole."

"Want me to break his kneecaps?" Dad asked, deadpan. I knew—just knew—that he was channeling a character from his favorite show about the mob. It was in the way he suddenly had a New Jersey drawl.

To my surprise, Tally giggled. "No. But it's sweet of you to offer."

Dad looked a little miffed that his vengeful offer had been called "sweet," but he nodded and leaned against the counter, crossing his legs at the ankles.

"Anyway, she called me after the breakup, and I went over to her place, and one thing led to another and..." I trailed off, hoping they'd extrapolate from there.

Mom beamed. "So romantic."

Guilt twisted in my gut like a knife. I really shouldn't lie to them. But they were so pleased, and now I couldn't stand the thought of disappointing them. Better to just pretend to break up down the road and tell them we'd decided we were meant to be friends, not lovers.

Finally, I turned to Tally, acknowledging her furious glare. Silently, I implored her to just go along with this for a while. We could fix it later. My parents had dropped hints over the years that I might like to settle down, but I hadn't realized just how much joy it would bring them if I did.

Tally tilted her head to the side, capitulating, but her expression told me that we would be having words later. Stern words.

"Should we eat before dinner gets cold?" Dad suggested. "We can talk over the meal."

"Sounds good." I waited for each of them to grab a plate before following them to the glass dining table.

Mom and Dad sat at the far end and the left side. Tally sat on the right, so I took the chair kitty corner to her, at the nearest end of the table. She tossed her long hair over her shoulder and a wave of sweet-scented air drifted toward me.

I peeked at her out of the corner of my eye. How would it feel to actually be dating her? To know that this beautiful woman, who'd always made me smile, was mine?

A surprising sense of satisfaction rippled through me. Strange. Did I actually like the idea of dating Tally?

I'd always known she was pretty, and it hadn't taken long to learn that she was kind and capable too. Those were good qualities in a friend, but I'd never allowed myself to think more on the matter than that.

Now, I found myself uncertain of what to do or how to act.

She was mad at me. Meanwhile, I was in the midst of a crisis and potentially having some more-than-friendly thoughts about my best friend. Like, would she smell sweet and fruity if I buried my face in the crook of her neck? Would her eyes burn in a different way if I dared to kiss her?

I tuned back into the conversation just in time to hear Mom say, "...know it's a bit premature, but we've always thought of you as part of the family."

Tally's eyes were panicked, her smile forced. Mom and Dad must have noticed, but perhaps they chalked it up to nerves and that's why they were going so far out of their way to make it clear they approved.

Unfortunately, Tally was blatantly uncomfortable and my mood soured. What had I been thinking, pressuring her into this? She was going through enough without me adding another layer of complication.

I set my cutlery down. "Mom, Dad, there's something I need to tell you. We aren't actually—"

"Going to be here during bye week." Tally cut me off. "Because Alec is coming to Lake's wedding in Hawaii with me."

I frowned at her. I'd been about to give her a way out. Why had she stopped me?

But she didn't make eye contact, just sliced into her steak after jabbing her fork into a juicy piece of it.

"What a perfect way to spend the break," Mom exclaimed.

"Just make sure not to let your training slip," Dad added, his tone implying that he was being one hundred percent serious for once.

"I won't." I'd worked too hard to earn my place on the team to lose it over a measly few days off.

"Speaking of hockey," he continued, pointing the tip of his knife at me. "Let's talk about that righteous goal you scored today."

The conversation shifted away from our supposed new relationship to focus on the game we all loved. Dad had opinions as always, and I listened to them with a grain of salt because while he was undoubtedly a legend, he'd also played in a different time—and a different position. Some things he said would be helpful, and others, less so.

Once we'd finished eating, Tally started clearing the dishes away.

"I'll help," I said, rising to my feet.

"No, no, I've got it," Mom said, sending Dad a meaningful look and nudging him with her elbow. "You can clean up next time."

I frowned. Clearly, something was going on.

I waited as Mom got up to help Tally. When Dad and I were alone, he leaned across the table, resting on his forearms.

"I'm glad you and Tally are giving this thing a shot." He kept his voice low, so they wouldn't hear him from the kitchen. "We really think she's the girl for you; no pressure, but we'd love to have her as a daughter-in-law."

The knife blade of guilt twisted again. I should admit the truth, but he looked so earnest and I couldn't bring myself to do it.

When Mom and Tally returned, Mom and Dad exchanged the kind of speaking glance only people who knew each other inside out could. She tilted her head slightly toward me and he responded with the faintest of nods, then checked his watch and said they'd better get home before they turned into pumpkins.

"Do you need a ride back to your apartment?" Mom asked Tally as she fished the car keys from her pocket and twirled them around her finger.

Tally glanced at me. "No, thanks, Mrs. W. I brought my car over earlier. It's parked down the block."

Dad waggled his eyebrows. Mom looked delighted.

We walked them to the door and I watched as they got into their car and drove away, wishing that I could stand on the porch all night, where Tally wouldn't be able to lay into me. Eventually, I closed the door and turned to face my fate.

Her arms were crossed over her chest, her foot tapping impatiently, and she gave me the evil eye. "Why did you make them think we're together for real?"

"I didn't mean to." My cheeks were hot, and I had no doubt

they were blazing red. I had the kind of complexion that showed my blushes easily. "I was trying to explain when you came back in, and they leapt to conclusions."

"And you didn't correct them because...?"

I shrunk under her glare. "They seemed so happy, and I didn't want to ruin it."

She sighed, and her arms dropped to her sides. "I don't like lying to them, but they did seem really pleased."

"Weirdly so, right?" I asked, scratching the back of my head.

She nodded and her gaze raked down my body as if she were evaluating me, wondering what made my parents think we'd be the "perfect couple".

I drew in a lungful of air. "I hate to ask, but do you mind just going along with it for a little while?"

She nodded again. "If I minded, I'd have let you set the record straight when you tried to during dinner." She shifted her weight from one leg to the other, the curve of her hip popping out and drawing my gaze. "Let's just do what we can to make this as painless as possible."

Relieved, I reached out to her. She took my hand and let me pull her into a hug.

"Everything will work out fine," I promised, breathing in the sweetness of tropical fruit with an underlying hint of chocolate.

"I hope so." She held me tighter. "I don't want anything to ruin this."

"Then we won't let it."

Somehow, I suspected it wouldn't be that simple, but I'd gotten us into this mess, so I'd get us out of it again, whatever it took.

"I have to go too," she said, stepping away from me. "I need to work tomorrow, to make sure the shop is stocked for Monday."

"Early start?" I asked.

"Nah, not too bad." She drew her keys from her pocket. "I'll see you later in the week. Train hard and stay safe."

I patted her arm as she walked past me, hoping the touch would reassure her. She let herself out and I waited until I heard her car door slam and saw the headlights flash before locking the door behind her.

As I wandered back to the living room, at loose ends about what to do with myself, my phone buzzed. I checked the screen and noticed that I had a message from my sister.

Jane: *How long have you been dating Tally and why did no one tell me?*

SEVEN

TALLY

Excitement fluttered in my stomach as I stood in the bright, airy lobby of Tranquility Bay Resort. Even inside, the air smelled of the sea, and through the windows, fluffy white clouds floated in a sky as blue as the cerulean waters we'd flown over before our flight landed an hour earlier.

I hadn't been sure what to expect of the resort. The photographs on the website had made it look lovely, but I knew better than to trust images that could easily have been manipulated or were simply out of date.

I'd been wrong to suspect them of misleading customers though. Even from what little I'd seen of the resort as we'd pulled up outside and handed our suitcases over to a bellhop, I could tell that the buildings were modern but had character and the exterior was lush with greenery.

Dare I hope I might even enjoy my time here?

"It's nice, isn't it?" Alec said from beside me. We were lined up at a large wooden desk, waiting for the receptionist to check us in.

"I'm excited to see the other side." I hadn't been able to tell from the website whether the coast adjoining the resort was sandy or rocky.

"Me too."

Nearby, there was a ping and the elevator doors opened. A couple stepped out, the woman's sandals slapping against the patterned vinyl floor. My brain glitched, refusing to fully register what I was seeing:

Coral, in a pretty, wrap around dress, with a white plumeria flower tucked behind her ear and glossy pink lips.

Beside her, Thad, in Hawaiian print board shorts and a white open-collared shirt, a lei around his neck.

Fuck my life. I'd been hoping to have more of a reprieve before coming face-to-face with them.

Their fingers were intertwined. They looked good together, I couldn't deny it. They fit in ways he and I never had.

Something touched my back and I flinched, relaxing when I realized it was Alec. He wound his arm around my waist and pulled me against his side. My hand instinctively came to rest on his chest so I could steady myself, and my eyes widened slightly at the firmness of the muscle beneath my palm.

Don't get used to him holding you like this, I warned myself. *Don't creep on him either.*

Thad spotted us first. He set a course straight for us, dragging Coral with him. She resisted, trying to tug him the other way. When he refused to be budged, her shoulders slumped, and she rolled her eyes and let him lead her over.

"I heard that you two had gotten together," Thad said, his dark gaze flicking between us. "I figured people must have gotten it wrong."

Alec's arm reflexively tightened around me. "Not only are we together, but we're solid." His lips brushed my temple and I barely resisted the urge to melt into his embrace. "I'm not stupid enough to repeat your mistake and lose her. I know Tally is precious and I'm man enough to hold onto her."

Thad glowered. "Masculinity has nothing to do with it. I saw a better option and went for it."

I tried to meet Coral's eyes, wondering what she made of all of this, but she was making it impossible to catch her gaze. She was obviously uncomfortable. My instincts were to smooth the situation over, but my lingering hurt and bitterness stopped me from taking any steps to do so.

Coral had created this awkwardness. She deserved to experience it fully.

"Better?" Alec snorted. "'Better' people don't stab their family in the back."

I wondered if I should open my mouth and say something about how we could all just be nice and get through this week peacefully, but my lips remained sealed.

Apparently, I had a petty streak.

Thad started to stalk away, his hand still joined with Coral's, but strangely, she hesitated.

"Tally, I..."

"Don't worry about it." I shook my head, dismissing her. I'd been silly to try to catch her gaze. Now that she seemed to want to talk, my chest was so tight that I didn't think I'd be capable of getting anything out.

"No, really, I—"

"Just go!" I snapped, losing my cool.

She flinched and slunk away, as if I'd been the one to hurt her and not the other way around.

"What was that about?"

I started, realizing we were now at the front of the line. The receptionist waved us over, his eyes sparkling with interest.

"That was my ex," I explained, grimacing. "He's here with

the same wedding party as me. The girl with him is my cousin, who he cheated on me with."

His golden forehead creased with sympathy. "Oh, honey. I'm sorry. That's rough."

"It's fine," I said, trying to come across as breezy but I had a suspicion I was falling short. "I've got my new man here."

May as well start the act now, right?

"So you do." He grinned and thrust his hand across the desk. "Alec Wright, right?"

Alec blinked in surprise. Hesitantly, he shook the man's hand. "Yeah. That's me."

"I'm such a fan." The receptionist held onto him for a few seconds longer than necessary, unable to tear his eyes from Alec's face. "The Dragons are my favorite team."

"Really?"

The guy laughed. "I know; it's not very Hawaiian of me to like ice hockey, but my Dad is from Montreal, and he's obsessed. He loves the Canadiens, so of course, I had to pick a different team to support. It drives him crazy that I chose one from the U.S."

"Sounds like you're a man of good taste," I said, relieved at him for offering such an easy change of topic from the shit show that was my former love life. "Who's your favorite player?"

He pursed his lips. "Promise not to hold it against me if it's not Alec Wright?"

Alec chuckled. "My ego isn't that massive."

"Phew!" He pretended to wipe sweat from his brow. "I love Badagova. He's such a machine."

I was impressed by his choice. A lot of people overlooked the defense and tended to favor the goal-scorers, but Davi Badagova was a total badass.

Someone cleared their throat behind us, and the receptionist straightened.

"Anyway, sorry to take up your time," he said briskly. "Let's get you all sorted then."

Five minutes later, we had two key cards in hand and our new receptionist friend wished us luck as we headed for the elevator. Our room was on the third floor, so I swiped the card and pushed the button to take us there.

I half-expected Alec to ask me if I was okay after our run-in with Coral and Thad, but perhaps he'd decided it was best not to mention anything that might ruin my mood, because he stayed quiet.

We followed the directions to room 324 and I pressed the card to the electronic reader by the handle, waited for the green light to flash, and opened the door.

Through the window opposite us, the ocean glimmered turquoise as it stretched into the horizon. Gauzy curtains softened the view, but it wasn't the riot of greens and blues that captured my attention.

It was the bed.

Singular.

As in, there was one bed.

The bottom dropped out of my stomach. It was at most a queen, with just enough room for a couple who didn't mind getting nice and cozy but not at all enough space for a woman who was trying her hardest not to be enticed by her absolutely gorgeous best friend. It certainly wasn't large enough for him to feel comfortable with the situation.

Oh god, would he think I'd done this on purpose?

"I'm sorry." I turned to him, tears stinging my eyes. "I swear it didn't cross my mind that we might have to share a bed. I'm so stupid. I should have called and asked to change my room to a double. Now we're stuck and the sign out front said no vacancy."

"Hey, cocobug. Take a breath." Alec guided me to the bed

and I perched awkwardly on the edge of it. "It's all right. We'll manage."

"But this is all my fault. If I'd been thinking clearly, I'd have remembered to plan ahead, but I just... I just..." I squeezed my eyes shut, so angry with myself for being overwhelmed and failing to do something as simple as changing the room booking so Alec wouldn't feel obligated to share a bed with me.

"It's not a big deal," he said quietly.

But it was. At least, it felt that way to me.

I looked around, desperately searching for a solution. There was no pull-out couch. We could potentially ask for one at reception but what if someone overheard and then our whole deception fell apart?

"I'll sleep on the ottoman," I declared, grateful to the idea for springing into my mind. It wasn't as good as a couch, but it would do.

He snorted. "Don't be ridiculous."

I glared at him. "I'm not. I'm trying to fix this."

His expression softened. "We're adults. We can share the bed without it having to be a big deal."

Could we? Because honestly, it seemed like a big deal.

Alec was sexy. Right now, he was serving as my white knight. I could retain a shred of control over myself while I was conscious, but once I fell asleep, there was every chance I'd wrap myself around him like an octopus.

"What if I cuddle you in my sleep?" I asked. "I'm a cuddler. I can't help it."

There. I'd set up a little plausible deniability in case I found myself drawn to him while asleep.

His lips quirked with amusement. "Tally, it isn't as if we haven't cuddled before. I'm sure we'll survive."

Perhaps, but would my heart emerge unscathed?

"Would you like me to sleep on the ottoman?" he offered, and the guilt settled inside me like a leaden weight.

"No, of course not. You're a professional athlete. You need a proper bed." Not to mention that he was doing so much for me already.

"I won't sleep in the bed if it's going to cause you this much stress."

I sighed. "I'm being dramatic, aren't I?"

He held up his thumb and finger an inch apart. "Only a little."

"Fine," I relented. "We can share the bed."

But I couldn't shake the feeling that our ruse had gotten off to a rocky start, and that this might be an omen of things to come.

EIGHT

ALEC

I knocked firmly on Mr. and Mrs. Dufresne's hotel room door and waited for them to answer. Tally had been anxious about seeing her parents in person for the first time since we'd decided to go ahead with this ruse, so we'd opted to drop by and visit them before dinner to get it out of the way.

Mrs. Dufresne—who tried to insist I call her Daisy every time we met—opened the door with a wide, infectious smile.

"Darling!" she exclaimed, sweeping Tally into a lavender-scented mom-hug. "How was the flight?"

"All smooth and on time," Tally replied, briefly returning the hug and then drawing back enough to meet her gaze. "How about yours?"

The Dufresnes had flown in yesterday morning, so Mrs. Dufresne could participate in a one-day yoga retreat happening nearby.

"A few bumps, but nothing to worry about, and the retreat was divine. I had the best time, and learned a new modification for one of my favorite poses." She leaned closer and lowered her voice. "Sometimes these things become necessary as we age. But shh, I'm still young at heart."

"Don't hog them, Daisy," Mr. Dufresne called from deeper inside the room. "Come in, kids. Are you unpacked? Do you have everything you need?"

"Yes, sir," I said as Daisy stepped aside, allowing Tally and I to enter. I debated whether to take Tally's hand or not. We hadn't discussed exactly what we were telling her parents—another oversight. I started to move away from her, certain that more deception was exactly what she wouldn't want, but to my surprise, she slipped her hand into mine.

"Oh, yes. We heard about that development from your mother," Mr. Dufresne said, eyeing our joined hands.

"It's still early, but we feel good about the decision to see if our friendship might turn into more," Tally said so naturally that I had to resist the urge to turn and stare at her.

Okay. Perhaps I hadn't given any thought as to what we were telling her parents, but apparently, she had.

"Yay." Mrs. Dufresne clapped, but then her smile faded. "I'm not sure if you've heard, but that snake Thad is here with Coral."

"I know." Tally's voice didn't give away how upset she'd been to see them earlier. "We ran into them downstairs."

"That jackass has some nerve," Mr. Dufresne snapped, his eyes glinting dangerously. "I'm amazed Sylvia allowed Coral to invite him."

Mrs. Dufresne's nose crinkled. "It's Lake's special day, which means she gets the final word, not Sylvia, however much my sister might wish otherwise. Lake said it was okay. I suppose she didn't want to alienate Coral."

"But it's okay to alienate Tally?" Mr. Dufresne demanded, his sharp expression reminding me of what a shark he was said to be in the courtroom.

Mrs. Dufresne waved her hand dismissively. "I'm not condoning it. Just explaining to Tally and Alec how it happened. If I'd known..."

"You would have complained to Aunt Sylvia, who'd have complained to Lake, who's stressed out enough already," Tally said, as if she'd already thought of all of this before. "It'll be fine. Right, Alec?"

"Yeah." I squeezed her hand. As far as I was concerned, my primary job for this weekend was to make her time here as bearable as possible and ensure that neither Thad nor Coral had the opportunity to hurt her any more than they already had.

I was her designated fake boyfriend bodyguard.

Tally sat on one end of the bed. Her parents' room was similar to ours, except that where we had a view of the water, their window overlooked a lush area of planting and rock gardens.

"Congratulations, you two," Mrs. Dufresne said belatedly. "We're so thrilled that you're together."

"We can't say we were waiting for it to happen, but we aren't surprised that it did," Mr. Dufresne added, his features relaxing again, losing their hard edges.

I glanced at Tally, wondering what was up with our parents. Both sets seemed to have half-expected us to eventually end up together.

We chatted for a while and then, once Tally had relaxed and we'd realized that we weren't going to have any issues with her parents, we returned to our room to prepare for dinner.

Those members of the bride and grooms' families who'd already arrived had been asked to gather at the waterfront restaurant to share a meal. I hoped Lake had the sense to keep us away from Coral and Thad.

"Maybe we should order room service and stay here," Tally

said as the door clicked shut behind us. "If we go, it's only going to create drama."

I hesitated. "Is that what you really want?"

If it was, then we'd do it, but I doubted the thought was anything more than a desperate desire to hide rather than an actual choice she wanted to make.

"No." She released a slow breath and flopped onto the bed. "If I do, he'll think he's won. I'd just rather avoid the unpleasantness."

"Let's make sure you look even more beautiful than usual then." Excitement churned in my gut as I opened the closet and withdrew one of the garment bags I'd hung in there earlier. I passed it to her and she took it, her head cocked curiously. "Open it."

I held my breath, praying that she liked my surprise.

She unzipped the garment bag and her breath hitched. "Oh, my God. You didn't have to do this!" Despite her protest, she stroked the pink dress, clearly pleased. "You spent so much on me already."

"I didn't get the shoes, but the matching purse is somewhere in there," I said, not addressing her comment.

She turned to me, her eyes shining with moisture. "This really wasn't necessary."

"But do you like it?" I asked, because that was all that mattered.

She clutched it to her chest. "I love it."

I allowed myself to breathe properly again. "Then put it on and let's wow everyone."

"Okay." Now that she'd accepted the gift for what it was, she squealed and pulled it gleefully from the bag. "It's such a pretty color."

"It is." It perfectly matched the pinkness of her cheeks

anytime she blushed. Not that I was stupid enough to say as much.

Practically bouncing, she took the dress into the bathroom to change. Meanwhile, I chose a pair of tidy slacks and a relatively tame white-and-blue patterned shirt. I slipped my feet into sandals and checked my reflection in the full-length mirror to make sure I looked good. I wanted Tally to be proud to have me on her arm, even if it wasn't real.

I relaxed against the pile of pillows on the bed and waited. And waited. And eventually, Tally emerged from the bathroom, not only wearing the pink dress with the purse in her hand, but also standing slightly taller than usual in black, strappy-heeled sandals that wrapped around her shapely calves. Her lips were painted pink, her cheeks dusted with blush, and dark eyeliner exaggerated the blue of her irises.

I couldn't look away. "You are... stunning."

She beamed. "You look good too."

I blinked and did my best to gather myself. "Are you ready to head down?"

She nodded. "Let me just grab a jacket in case it gets cold."

She fished around in her suitcase for a jacket, slung it over her arm and offered me her other arm to escort her out of the room.

"Is this too much?" she asked as we waited for the elevator, gesturing to her dress, shoes, and makeup.

"A situation like this calls for the big guns," I assured her.

When she didn't look comforted, I realized I was going to have to do better. I dipped my head, so my mouth was near her ear, not wanting my next words to be overheard by any passersby.

"Any guy who sees you in that dress is going to want to put his hands on you. Touch you. Taste you. Ruck up your skirt and see if you're as scorching hot as you look."

An image slammed into me. Tally, pressed against the wall while I edged up the hem of her pretty dress and caressed the silken skin of her thigh.

Would she lean into my touch? Whimper as I moved my hand higher? Part her legs to give me better access?

My cock stiffened.

Fuck. Get yourself together.

But the image wouldn't budge from my mind.

"This dress may look proper but with you inside it, wrapped up like a tempting package, trust me, it's anything but," I added.

She stared at me, her eyes wide, her cheeks painted the same shade of pink as the dress, just as I'd pictured. Sparks of need zapped through me everywhere we touched.

How had I never realized exactly how hot my best friend was?

The elevator pinged and opened.

I cleared my throat. "Come on. We'd better get down there."

She followed me into the elevator, her eyes slightly glazed. Perhaps my misguided attempt to reassure her had affected her as strongly as it had me.

Neither of us spoke as we rode the elevator down, gathering another pair of guests on the second floor before reaching the lobby. Signs directed us to the waterfront restaurant, and when we reached it, I paused to admire the view.

The restaurant projected out over the water and the sides were open. The roof was made of some kind of thatched material, and a waterfall rose behind the building, spotted with greenery and tiny pink flowers. It looked natural, but surely, it must be man-made. It was too odd a location for a naturally occurring waterfall.

Rectangular tables were positioned end-to-end along the

center of the part of the restaurant nearest to the water. Our party was gathered there, chatting and laughing. The open air was warm, and birds chirped from somewhere out of sight.

I was relieved to see that Thad and Coral were seated at the nearest end of the tables, with Lake and her fiancé, while the empty chairs were all at the opposite end.

We greeted the happy couple. I shot a warning look at Thad, and noticed that I wasn't the only one to do so. Coral did as well. We managed to escape without Tally's ex saying a word, which was better than I'd hoped for.

We claimed a pair of seats opposite two men I didn't know. I pulled a chair out for Tally, and she smiled at them as she sat. We exchanged greetings.

"How do you know the bride and groom?" she asked them, reaching for the ice water and filling both our glasses.

"Chris is an old college friend of ours," the guy opposite Tally said, his gaze locked on her as if he'd just seen an angel.

My eyelid twitched. Yes, I'd just finished telling her how irresistible she was in that dress, but I hadn't realized I'd have to scare off horny guys quite this soon.

"I thought the dinner tonight was for family," I said tersely.

Tally elbowed me.

The guy just laughed. "It was supposed to be, but Lake's family is bigger than Chris's, so he invited us to make up numbers. I'm Jackson, and this is Ben."

"Tally," she replied, stretching her hand across the table. "Short for Tallulah."

He accepted her hand with a flourish. I narrowed my eyes. If he kissed it, I'd be forced to kick him under the table. Tally and I might not actually be together, but for the purposes of this wedding, everyone had to think that we were.

"That's an interesting name," Jackson said.

I coughed. "I'm Alec."

"Right winger for the Colorado Dragons." The words burst from Ben as if he'd been holding them back since the start of the conversation. His face turned red. He had one of those freckled complexions that meant when he blushed, he did it with his whole body. "I love hockey. I play in a rec league."

"Oh, yeah? What position are you?" I asked.

"Center."

"Nice." There had been a time when I'd thought I might like to be center but then I learned I prefer to zip around the sides of the ice and slip past the goalie rather than launch head-on attacks.

"So, how do you know Chris and Lake?" Jackson asked. His gaze still hadn't left Tally.

"Lake is my cousin," she said.

He turned to Alec. "And you?"

Ah. I got it. He wanted to know if we were related or here as a couple. As if me pulling out her chair hadn't been indication enough.

"I'm Tally's boyfriend." I stared him down and he seemed to get the hint. "She's my little cocobug."

Jackson raised an eyebrow.

Tally laughed. "I'm a chocolatier. I've always been obsessed with chocolate, so he's called me that since we were in school together."

"You guys have been together for that long?" Ben looked surprised. "I never realized Alec had a partner. I feel like you've never mentioned her in any interviews."

"We were best friends," I explained, subtly letting Jackson know that he had no chance of snatching Tally away from me. "We only confessed our feelings for each other recently."

"I love chocolate." Jackson didn't seem as deterred as he ought to be. "Especially if there's caramel involved."

Tally's face lit up. "Such a good combination. Especially if it's dark chocolate and there's a little sea salt or something to cut through the sweetness."

He grinned at her. "Exactly."

She grinned back.

I gritted my teeth. I liked chocolate, but I didn't have the same enthusiasm for it that she did, and right now, that felt glaringly obvious.

"What about you?" I asked Ben, hoping to shift the conversation. "What food do you like?"

He shrugged. "All of it."

Well, that wasn't exactly helpful.

"Do you work in a chocolate factory?" Jackson asked Tally.

"No, I own a shop." As she explained how she'd bought Coco Luxe two years ago and had begun operating it with just her and an assistant, Jackson was completely riveted.

It irritated me.

Of course I wanted people to be interested in Tally. Realistically, I should be pleased about the attention because it showed what a fool Thad had been to let her go, but I couldn't help feeling that Jackson needed to mind his own business.

After all, we couldn't have him messing up our ruse.

We chatted through our main course. Jackson and Ben were surprisingly good company, even if I didn't like the way Jackson's whole body seemed to orientate itself to Tally.

Then dessert arrived.

It was, unfortunately for me, a trio of chocolate.

Between the flight and everything else, I'd hardly exercised today, so I couldn't afford to eat it. Neither Tally nor Jackson had any such compunction. Tally savored every bite of the brownie, mousse, and truffle. Rapture stole across her face as she chewed and Jackson looked like he was about to cream his pants.

Fucking hell.

Jackson picked up his own remaining truffle and offered it to Tally. She smiled at him and reached for it, but I beat her there, snatching it from between his fingers and popping it into her mouth. Her eyes widened as her lips closed over my fingers and I groaned at the silken slide.

Behind my slacks, my cock woke up. I breathed as evenly as I could and considered whether spilling ice water on my lap might be the best way to get myself under control.

Waitstaff began to remove the plates and glasses, and somewhere behind us, music started. A group of younger cousins jumped up and headed for the small dance area attached to the restaurant.

"Want to dance?" I asked Tally, thinking that it would be a great way to get her away from her new friend.

She nibbled her lower lip. "I don't know…"

"It'll show up Thad," I murmured.

Her jaw set and her lips firmed. "Let's do it."

I grinned, telling myself that my enthusiasm was all about protecting my friend and not about the fact I was about to get to hold her in my arms.

NINE

TALLY

I placed my hand in Alec's and let him lead me onto the uncovered wooden dance floor adjoining the restaurant. A surge of something like electricity zapped between us and I bit my lower lip to stop myself from gasping.

My fingertips tingled as he firmed his grip on me, as if they were desperate to touch more of him. They wanted to journey up his muscular arms and discover all of the parts of him I'd never experienced before.

This is a dangerous game you're playing.

I hoped like hell that I wouldn't come to regret it. If I lost Alec, I'd be crushed. He was more than just a friend. He was the most important person in my life.

The song changed to something upbeat with an acoustic guitar and a rapidly beating drum. Alec guided me around until I was standing chest-to-chest with him. Or close to it, considering I was quite a bit shorter than him.

We began to move. We'd danced together many times before, so I knew he had good rhythm, but we'd always maintained a certain level of distance between us. Now, he erased that space, moving closer to me each time we swayed until his hand came to rest on my hip and my breasts brushed against him each time we moved.

My nipples tightened and I sucked in a breath, hoping he wouldn't notice. I was wearing a strapless bra beneath the dress, so fortunately, my reaction shouldn't have been obvious.

It's just friction, I told myself. *Friction causes a physiological response.*

It was easier to believe that than to admit to myself that my best friend's touch turned me on.

I closed my eyes, trusting him to keep me safe and hoping that the visual barrier would stop my unwanted physical reaction to him. But not being able to see him merely amplified the current between us, causing the hair on my arms to stand on end with each accidental caress.

Heat pooled low in my core as Alec twirled me. He smelled of lemon, sea salt, and man. Delicious and unique and so tantalizing that I wanted to bury my face in his chest and breathe him in.

Opening my eyes, I blinked up at him hazily while my vision cleared. His dark gaze stared back at me, never wavering. His tattooed arm flexed ever so slightly around me and his hold on my waist tightened.

"Tally, I—"

The song ended and, suddenly, Thad was standing beside us.

Alec turned to him and growled, "What do you want?"

Thad puffed his chest out. He looked ridiculous, trying to posture in front of the wall of muscle that was my best friend. While Thad wasn't a limp noodle, he could never match Alec in size or sheer intimidation power.

"Stop embarrassing yourselves," he said snidely. "You're

obviously faking this whole thing so that Tally doesn't look like a loser, but we can all see through the act."

I froze. My stomach hardened and my chest constricted as I temporarily forgot how to breathe.

Was it true?

Did everyone know we were pretending?

Were they gossiping behind my back?

I never should have gone along with this. It was a stupid idea. Alec had meant well, but I was the one who would end up paying for our bad decisions.

Coral appeared behind Thad and yanked on his arm.

"What are you doing?" she hissed, flashing me an apologetic look.

Thad folded his arms. "I just want Tally to admit the truth."

"Why do you care?" she demanded. "It isn't any of your business."

But Thad didn't budge.

I risked a glance at Alec, scared to see what his reaction to this confrontation would be. His jaw was set, his expression thunderous, his eyes so dark they surely spelled Thad's doom. I shivered.

Alec squared up to Thad. Though my ex was tall, Alec was a good inch taller, and he outweighed Thad by forty pounds. He'd also been in far more fights than Thad had.

My insides fluttered with anticipation. Dear God, was I excited by the idea of Alec handing Thad his ass?

Alec leaned over him, and when he spoke, his voice was a low rumble. "I know this is a wedding and we're all supposed to play nice, but if you ever disrespect my girl again, you'll be seeing stars for a week."

Thad's eyes widened and he instinctively stepped back. When he realized he was visibly backing down, he scowled and made a show of scraping his foot against the floorboards, as if he'd slipped or tripped rather than simply been intimidated by a bigger, stronger man.

"You won't lay a finger on me," he sneered. "You wouldn't risk your job."

Privately, I agreed. Any altercation Alec ended up in could impact his career. The NHL didn't mind its players fighting on the ice, but it preferred they not throw fists when they were off it.

Alec's steely glare didn't waver. "Some things are worth it. Tally is abso-fucking-lutely one of those things."

"She's just a friend," Thad protested. "You don't care about her that much."

"See, that's where you're wrong. There's very little I care about more than her. Not hockey. I love the sport, but I don't need to worry about my job. I have enough money to retire tomorrow and live in comfort. So if you think concern about my career will stop me from defending my girl, then you're wrong."

A kernel of worry began to form in the pit of my gut. He sounded a bit too convincing. Alec wouldn't actually do anything to throw his career away because of me, would he?

I couldn't let him. I never should have gone along with this ruse in the first place.

"Alec," I said, laying my hand on his arm. "Perhaps we should—"

"Admit it's fake?" Thad suggested, his voice higher and less confident than before.

Without taking his eyes off Thad, Alec said, "Does this look fake?"

And then he turned and kissed me.

He caught me off guard and I gasped against his lips, which were firm on mine.

At first, the kiss was chaste. Alec was making a point. But

then he softened and drew me against his body, cupping the back of my head with one of his big hands.

I tilted my face, angling myself closer. I wanted more.

His tongue brushed along the seam of my lips and I shuddered and parted them for him. He delved inside, his tongue caressing mine. A groan tore from him and he pressed himself tighter against me.

Something stiff and insistent throbbed against my belly.

Oh, God. He was hard.

My best friend was kissing me, and he liked it so much that he'd gotten hard. Was this a dream?

I pretended not to notice, worried that drawing attention to the situation in his pants might stop this glorious, all-consuming kiss. He tasted of sugar-free soda. His fingertips dug into the soft flesh of my hips and I whimpered.

He released me. My eyes flew open and I gazed up into his. They were almost black, his pupils blown out. His breath came in ragged bursts.

I searched his face, wondering what he was thinking and how much of that had been real. It was too raw to have all been a show, wasn't it?

A whistle pierced the air, and we leapt apart.

I looked around. Thad and Coral had gone, but we'd drawn quite an audience.

"Let's go to our room," I suggested, immediately blushing when I realized that he might think I was coming onto him. "Before there's any more drama, I mean. Not for anything else. You know I—"

His expression eased into a smile. "I know, cocobug. Let's get out of here. We've had enough excitement for one night."

He wound his arm around me, the embrace as comfortable as ever. I tried to sense if there was any tension in his muscles, and whether he'd been as shaken by our kiss as I was, but he seemed completely at ease. Meanwhile, I wanted to wrap my legs around his waist and demand more.

It's only fake, I reminded myself. *He isn't yours. He doesn't want you. Not like that.*

But I couldn't help recalling what he'd said to Thad. None of it had come across as false or exaggerated. He truly cared for me that deeply, so perhaps there was hope for more.

We returned to the table. Mom and Dad were sitting opposite Chris and Lake now, chatting about their plans for tomorrow. I heard something about beach volleyball but I was too riddled with nerves to make any sense of it without context.

"We're off to our room," I said when they fell quiet for a moment.

Mom frowned. "Is everything okay?"

I glanced at Lake. If none of them had noticed the confrontation with Thad, then I was hardly about to mention it. "Yeah. Just tired. I'll see you tomorrow."

"You too, darling. Sweet dreams."

I hugged Mom and then Dad. As we turned away from the table, Jackson waved at me and I waved back. He was a nice guy.

The journey to our room didn't take long. Once inside, I took my pajamas to the bathroom, locked the door, and stripped off the beautiful dress Alec had bought for me.

I smiled to myself. I'd definitely have opportunities to wear it again. It was the sort of dress that could look completely different depending on what shoes, jewelry, and accessories I paired it with.

I changed into the pajamas and wiped my face clean of makeup, then slowly made my way out of the bathroom. It was still relatively early, but Alec was already in bed, the blankets around his waist, his muscular torso on display. Tattoos wound up his left side, around his shoulder, and down his arm to his wrist.

Ugh, why did he have to be so hot?

I looked at him and then at the ottoman. It really wouldn't be terrible to sleep on. It was long enough that I could lie down, I'd just need to curl my legs up. As long as I didn't move from my position, I wouldn't roll off the edge.

Shame I'd never been a very peaceful sleeper.

I nibbled my lower lip, torn. I didn't want to sleep on the ottoman. The bed looked far more comfortable. But Alec had just turned everything on its head. How was I supposed to lie next to him when I now knew the delicious friction of his body against mine, and when the scent of his skin would remind me of the wonderful kiss we'd shared?

It was only for show.

I had to remember that. Alec didn't really want me. The kiss had been part of the ruse. He didn't seem flustered by the idea of sleeping together at all, and he'd already pointed out the hypocrisy of my protests about snuggling earlier.

I had no reason not to get into that bed with him.

None—except my sanity.

Too bad my priorities were skewed.

Hesitantly, I pulled back the covers and slipped underneath. I kept a safe distance between us, internally debating whether to use one of the pillows as a divider. But that would seem silly. Over the top.

With a sigh, I flicked off the light and closed my eyes. I could get through this. Sharing a bed with Alec didn't have to be a big deal. He'd said as much himself.

"Good night," I murmured.

He rolled onto his side and faced away from me. "Night, cocobug."

I waited for sleep to claim me. Unfortunately, the minutes dragged on and I remained perfectly awake.

Eventually, Alec rolled onto his back. I started when his hand slipped into mine and gave a gentle squeeze.

"Everything will be okay," he promised in the dark.

"I know," I whispered, but it was a lie. I couldn't help feeling that everything was about to go very, very wrong.

Perhaps, in trying to protect my dignity, I'd endangered something even more precious: my heart.

TEN

ALEC

What the hell had I been thinking when I kissed Tally last night?

My feet thudded in the sand as I jogged along the beach around the corner from the Tranquility Bay Resort. The sky was clear and tinged with pink, the breeze crisp, and only two other solitary figures had ventured out this early in the morning.

Sand kicked up behind me, and I eyed the rocky outcrop I was running toward, then checked my exercise watch to see how many more miles I had to go before I'd clocked up my minimum for the day. Only another mile left. If I reached the outcrop, turned around and headed back to the resort, that should be about right.

I smiled at an elderly man strolling with his dog as I passed him. I could have opted to run on the treadmill in the resort's gym, but who in their right mind would do that when they could be out here in one of the most beautiful places I'd ever seen?

Memories of the kiss tugged at my mind. Seriously, what had I been thinking?

I'd wanted to make a point, and I'd succeeded, but I'd spent the whole damn night with a raging hard on. I'd dreamed that I'd followed Tally into the bathroom, peeled that sexy pink dress from her body, and fucked her until she couldn't do anything other than whimper, moan, and plead for more.

She was my *best friend*. I wasn't supposed to have those kinds of thoughts about her.

Of course, I'd always known she was pretty. It was obvious. Her clear blue eyes, long dark hair, and creamy skin reminded me of snow white, except Tally also possessed the kind of curves that drove men wild and plush lips that would look perfect wrapped around my cock.

For fuck's sake. I had to stop objectifying her. It had never been a problem before, so why now?

Because now you know she tastes as sweet as she looks.

The insidious whisper was perhaps the most honest I'd managed to be with myself. Previously, as long as I hadn't thought of Tally in sexual terms or done anything with her of that nature, I could pretend not to be affected by her, but with one kiss, I'd blasted my defenses to smithereens.

God, I hoped I hadn't fucked up our friendship.

The sun peeked over the horizon and I winced, shielding my gritty eyes from it.

Hopefully, Tally would wake up while I was gone, and when I returned, everything would be back to normal between us. If that didn't happen, I wasn't sure what I'd do. Things had been so tense between us last night. We'd both been trying to pretend nothing had happened, yet we'd failed to behave anything like normal.

I reached the outcrop, pivoted, and started back toward the

resort. Another handful of people had appeared on the beach. A pair of women were perched on lounge chairs and drinking coffees while a resort employee strung up volleyball nets.

I passed them by and made my way through the resort grounds, winding between rock pools and greenery until I reached the main building. I climbed the stairs to the second floor and followed the signs to the gym. I swiped my key card to enter and my spirit lightened as I left the gloom of the hallway for the bright airiness of the gym.

Floor to ceiling windows dominated one wall and treadmills were lined up in front of them. On the opposite side of the room, mirrors covered the respective space, so weightlifters could monitor their form as they worked out. A teenage girl was running on a treadmill and a guy with silver-flecked hair and a slight belly was doing bicep curls in the corner.

I started on the leg extensions. Hockey players need strong glutes and thigh muscles to skate quickly and powerfully around the ice. My quads were already warm from the run, so I was able to add weight quickly until I reached my limit.

I reconfigured the machine to do leg curls and lay on my stomach, hitching my heels beneath the bar so I could curl them back and exercise my hamstrings. I started at low weight and escalated. I was near my maximum when the gym door opened and Thad strode in.

My jaw clenched and my muscles twitched, almost causing me to lose my rhythm. Thad looked around and, when he saw me, his expression darkened. One of his hands clasped a drink bottle while the other fisted at his side. When he noticed my attention on it, he relaxed the fingers but it was too late. He'd already given away the fact he was about as pleased to see me as I was to see him.

To my surprise, he went straight to the other leg weight

machine and stacked on more plates than I thought wise. It was only when he assumed the same position as me and began pumping his legs that I realized he'd chosen the same amount of weight I was currently lifting in some misguided show of machismo.

Did the cocky asshole actually believe he could keep up with a professional athlete?

I added another ten pounds to my weights and started a new set of reps. A few seconds later, he followed suit.

My lip curled. He really was trying to show that he could keep up with me.

Never mind. I didn't have to play into his game. I finished my set and added another ten pounds, maxing out in the same place I usually did. When I was halfway through the set, Thad increased his weights too.

I rolled my eyes. The idiot was going to hurt himself.

I unloaded the leg curl and moved to the squat rack. A few seconds later, Thad claimed the second squat rack. This was ridiculous. He had to realize that I knew what he was doing. If he'd been serious about working his hamstrings, he'd have spent at least a couple more sets on the leg curl. Instead, he'd abandoned it to go head-to-head with me.

I started off light. Next to me, Thad scoffed and started with an additional fifteen pounds. My back teeth ground together and my nostrils flared as I breathed out, reminding myself not to let him get to me. My purpose here was to keep up my regular workout schedule, not to put Thad in his place.

Yet after one set, I found myself adding twenty pounds, so my bar outweighed his. It still wasn't a strain for me. He added another plate to each side of his barbell, edging me out. His breathing was heavy as he lowered himself into a squat and pushed back into the starting position.

I finished the set and stacked more weight on. Now, my breath started to come heavier too.

Thad grunted as he thrust the bar into place on the rack and tossed more on without even finishing the set. He glanced at me and our gazes met, a silent challenge in his.

I wasn't immature enough to let him drive me to not complete a set, but I did shift up again more quickly than I usually would have. I'd nearly reached my maximum usual weight, but my legs felt strong. I could go heavier.

Beside me, Thad was red-faced and sweating. His muscle shirt was soaked through, and his lanky limbs were beginning to shake.

"Give it up," I muttered, loud enough for him to hear but not for anyone else to. "I get paid to be fit. You're a finance guy. You can't beat me in this."

If he challenged me to a math test or quizzed me about shares and return rates, he'd come out on top, but this was my natural habitat. There was no shame in losing to a professional. But judging from his glower, he didn't see things that way.

Briefly, I considered setting my barbell aside and being the bigger person. I knew I could out-squat him. But then I recalled what he'd done to Tally and any sympathy I might have had for him fled.

I added more weight.

He did too.

I added more.

So did he.

And again, until finally, he added so much that he couldn't lift the barbell off the rack.

"I win," I said, and unloaded my barbell.

I left him collapsed on a bench, mopping his face on his shirt and trembling from head to toe.

Back in our hotel room, I stretched my legs thoroughly and

showered, then changed into a T-shirt and board shorts and went looking for Tally.

I found her at the waterfront restaurant, with an empty breakfast platter in front of her and goddamn Jackson from the night before seated opposite. I grabbed a chair, dragged it over, and draped my arm around her shoulders.

As far as Jackson knew, Tally was taken. He needed to back off.

"Are you done with breakfast, cocobug?" I asked, dropping a kiss on her cheek. "Morning, Jackson."

"Hey, Alec." Irritatingly, he didn't seem bothered by my presence.

Tally placed her empty coffee cup on her plate. "Yeah, I finished a while ago. We've just been chatting."

"Want to head back to the room and figure out our game plan for today?" I wanted nothing more than to get her away from her new friend. She'd had enough man trouble for one trip. The last thing she needed was some stranger lusting after her too.

"Um, okay sure. But don't you want something to eat too?"

I gritted my teeth. I hadn't thought of that, but she had a point. "Just give me a moment."

I went to the buffet and loaded a plate with eggs and hash, then filled a bowl with Greek yoghurt, granola, and fresh fruit. I carried both back to the table, sat, and dug into them with gusto, not because I was starving but because I wanted to get back to our room and away from Jackson as quickly as possible.

As I ate, Jackson and Tally made small talk about their siblings—or in Tally's case, her lack thereof, their parents, and their friends. Jackson apparently had two siblings, both older, and his parents were rich and semi-retired, gallivanting around the world on cruise ships and leading photography tours in some of the planet's most beautiful places.

It annoyed me that he seemed like an interesting person. I supposed, under normal circumstances, I should have been pleased that a friendly guy with a good job was showing interest in my best friend. He was a better match for her than Thad had been. But I couldn't bring myself to be grateful to him or even to envision them together.

For now, Tally was mine, and that was that.

I shoveled yoghurt, granola, and fruit into my mouth, chugging down water between mouthfuls. After only a few minutes, I cleared both my plate and bowl. I pushed back my chair and stood. Tally arched an eyebrow, obviously confused by my behavior. Frankly, I was too. Pretending to be her boyfriend was messing with me.

"I'll see you later," she said to Jackson, wiggling her fingers at him in a cute little wave.

"Bye, Tally," he said with a grin. "Bye, Alec."

As we walked back to our hotel room, I felt her eyes on me.

"What was that about?" she asked, jostling me with her elbow. "Is everything okay? You're acting a little strange."

I sighed. "I had a bit of a run in with Thad this morning."

"Oh." Her face fell. "I'm sorry."

Damn, now I'd made her feel bad.

"Don't be. It just threw me off a little."

"Hey!" The feminine call came from my right. I turned toward the sound. A tall, slim woman was hurrying toward us, gesturing for us to wait. She stopped in front of us. "It's Tally, right? Lake's cousin?"

"Yes." Tally regarded her curiously. "What's up?"

"There's volleyball happening on the beach around the side of the resort in ten minutes." She tucked a lock of dirty blonde hair behind her ear. "You guys should both come. Don't forget to wear your swimsuits."

She scurried away before either of us could reply.

"We don't have to go," I said, taking her hand and giving it a squeeze. "Especially not if it's going to make you uncomfortable. Coral will probably be there."

A range of expressions flitted across her face but then her jaw set. "We didn't come here to hide in our room. Let's go."

ELEVEN

What was going on with Alec?

He was behaving strangely. Sure, seeing Thad earlier today might explain some of it, but what about that weird scene with Jackson over breakfast? Alec had never been the most socially outgoing guy, but he wasn't usually rude.

For a few seconds, my heart skipped and I'd allowed myself to wonder if maybe this was how he behaved when he was jealous, but then I returned to the real world and realized that something else must be going on. Either that, or he was going all-in with the act.

We didn't speak again as we returned to our room. The air smelled faintly of lemon. He must have showered before joining me for breakfast and the scent had lingered.

Lake's friend had said to wear swimsuits. I'd packed two, and I wasn't sure how I felt about prancing around in either of them. Usually, I liked my body. It was strong and functional and had generous curves, but Thad had gotten in my head about my size. Coral was rail thin, and she'd no doubt wear her skimpiest bikini. Perhaps I should choose something more conservative.

I opened my suitcase and rummaged around until I'd found both the pale pink bikini and the black one-piece suit with a dark blue floral design wrapped around the side.

Alec looked over and frowned. "What are you doing?"

I shrugged. "Deciding which one to wear."

A furrow formed between his eyebrows. "Why? You love the bikini."

It was true. I did. It sat just perfectly to show off enough to be sexy without making me uncomfortable.

"I don't know." I dithered. "The one-piece might be more suitable."

His eyes narrowed. "Do you, or do you not, like the bikini better?"

"Yeah, but…" I trailed off, unsure how to finish the protest. But I feel self-conscious? But my ex is an asshole who's making me behave like an insecure teenager?

Alec dropped the tube of sunscreen he'd retrieved from his suitcase on the nightstand and circled around to me. He stood less than a foot from me and gazed steadily into my eyes.

"I say this as both a friend and a hot-blooded straight man. You look fucking delicious in that bikini."

I shivered, unable to tear my eyes from his. They scorched me to my soul, dark and heated and unlike anything I'd experienced before.

"If you want to wear the one-piece, then do it, but if you're having second thoughts because of a trash human who doesn't deserve you, then fuck that negativity and show us how gorgeous and confident you are in your own skin."

I straightened my back. "You're right."

"Of course I am." His fingertips grazed my hip, and I was grateful for the sweater because I was certain I was flushed from head to toe. His pupils had almost swallowed the chocolatey brown of his irises.

His desire looked so real. How was I supposed to remember that it wasn't?

He was playing his role to perfection.

"I'll be in the bathroom." I snatched up the bikini and fled.

I changed slowly, needing the time to rebuild my confidence. I hated that Thad had knocked it. With my dark hair and bright eyes, I knew I looked good. Not to mention the spectacular cleavage the bikini would reveal. Coral wasn't the only one who could rock a swimsuit.

My toiletries were set out on the vanity and I took my time to apply sunscreen. I'd brought a special one for my face since I was so pale that adding normal sunscreen tended to make me look like a ghost. This one, slightly tinted, would give me a little color.

I added a swipe of lip gloss—pink, to match the bikini—lined my eyes, and applied mascara.

There. The black eyeliner set off the blue of my eyes and the pink bikini made my complexion look like strawberries and cream rather than washed out.

I had this.

I knocked on the door to the bedroom. "Are you dressed?"

"Yeah," Alec called back.

I opened it and stepped through. He'd stripped off his T-shirt and was wearing just the board shorts and a pair of flip flops. His chest gleamed and I wondered, not for the first time, whether he waxed. He didn't seem the type, but it was very smooth.

"Can you sunscreen my back?" I asked, holding the bottle out.

"Sure." He took it from me. "Turn around."

I spun away from him and held my breath until the rough

pads of his fingers brushed my skin. He started with my lower back, rubbing lotion on in circular motions, and worked his way up, pausing between my shoulders to dig his thumb into a knot just inside my shoulder blade.

My eyelids drooped, and I forced myself to pull away. "Thanks."

"Are you sure I got you everywhere? I didn't finish your upper back."

"I got that part," I assured him, and it might be true. I'd certainly tried to do my own back, but honestly, if his hands were on me for one more second, I might find myself thinking some un-friend-like thoughts.

If I burned, I burned. At least I could apply aloe to soothe it. If I melted beneath Alec's touch and gave in to my growing desire to throw myself into his arms, the consequences would be far more severe.

"Can you take the room key card?" I asked. It wasn't as if I had any hidden pockets in my bikini to keep it in.

He nodded, and slipped the key card into the pocket of his board shorts, then he opened the door and held it for me.

As we wandered down the hall to the elevator, he looked over at me.

"Have you ever played volleyball before?" he asked.

"No. I'm hoping it's one of those things I can pick up as we go." I was reasonably coordinated, even if I wasn't what you'd call sporty. Provided someone explained the rules and the moves, I should be able to manage it easily enough.

"Traditionally, it's only two players per team," Alec explained as he pressed the button for the elevator. "We might play four to a team depending on how many are interested, or perhaps we'll rotate teams each time a certain number of points are scored."

"Okay." Small teams were both good and bad. They meant

I was less likely to get confused about what was going on, but if I was terrible, then whoever was on my team would be handicapped by my poor skill. "What are the rules?"

Alec talked through the basics as we rode the elevator down and wound our way through the resort to the beach. When we reached the sand, I kicked off my sandals and used my hand to shield my eyes as I scanned the beach for my cousins.

Coral, Lake, Chris, and Shanna, the other bridesmaid, were chatting beside one of the nets. Lake waved us over. Designer frames covered her eyes, and I couldn't help thinking that sunglasses had been a good idea. I'd left mine in our room.

"Hey, guys! Thanks for coming!" Lake tossed a ball in the air and caught it, grinning mischievously. "Half our group is still in bed—including the lazy groomsmen—but I wanted to get the volleyball going before it's so hot that all we want to do is swim. I thought we could have two teams of three. It's a little unconventional, but there are six of us and I don't want anyone missing out."

I glanced around, surprised to realize that Thad was nowhere in sight. A niggle of worry wormed through me. Alec hadn't done anything to him when he saw him earlier, had he?

"Coral and I have both played before," Lake continued. "So we'll each lead a team. Have either of you played?"

"Once or twice," Alec said.

I shook my head. "Not me."

She nodded, her fingers spreading across the sides of the ball. "So, we have two people with some experience and two with none. Excellent. I'll team up with Tally and Alec and Coral can play with Chris and Shanna."

I exchanged a look with Alec. She hadn't grouped us as I'd expected. It would make more sense for her to want to play with Chris, which would mean either splitting us up or switching assigned roles with Coral. Perhaps Lake had noticed our confrontation with Thad last night and was wary of putting Alec and I into close proximity with Coral.

"Everyone happy?" Lake asked.

We all nodded.

"Perfect." She bounced on the balls of her feet. "Let me run over the rules quickly."

While she talked, I tried to absorb as much information as possible, but between her rundown and the one I'd gotten from Alec, there was too much to cram into my mind. Surely it would make sense once we got started.

We split up into our respective teams and Lake joined us on the side of the net closest to the resort. She started with the ball, bopping it over. Coral hit it back. I was sure there were proper names for the movements but I didn't know what they were.

The ball flew toward me, so I formed a fist and tried to bounce it back the same way Coral had, but instead of crossing the net, it went straight up in the air and would have landed on our side if not for Lake.

"Let me show you how," Alec murmured, and suddenly he was behind me, his arms circling around my waist as he shifted my hands. "Like this."

"Thanks," I said breathlessly.

Next time the ball came over, I was able to do my part, but Alec didn't ease back. Instead, at every opportunity, he seemed to find a reason to put his hands on me. The scents of sunscreen and lemon filled my nose, and despite the warmth of the sand between my toes, all I could feel was the heat of Alec's body any time he drew close to me.

He was distracting as hell.

When Thad arrived, along with Jackson and Ben, and started watching from the sideline, the situation only got worse.

"Stop it," I hissed at Alec, pretending not to notice the way his eyes widened.

What did he expect? He was flustering me.

It's just part of his act, I reminded myself for the umpteenth time. *Don't fool yourself into thinking it means anything.*

Opposite us, Coral was on her best behavior. I noticed her sneaking peeks at Thad, and I also noticed Thad stealing glances at both her and me.

"Why does he keep looking over here?" I murmured to Alec as he corrected my stance before serving.

"Because you look hot as fuck," he said, and kissed my cheek.

Just. For. Show.

Alec made such a perfect fake boyfriend. It would be so easy to forget that none of it was real.

A ringing phone interrupted the game. Lake turned toward the sound and missed the ball. It landed on the sand and rolled toward me.

"Sorry." Alec pulled his phone from his pocket and checked the screen. "It's my agent. I'd better answer." He raised the phone to his ear and strode off the back of the court, putting distance between us so he could speak in private.

I tried not to feel like he was abandoning me. What if Coral or Lake—or god forbid, Thad—said something unpleasant while he was gone?

"Mind if I join?"

I jumped, caught off guard.

"We'd love that," Lake replied, smiling at Jackson, who'd magically materialized beside us. She rolled the ball across to Coral. "Do you know the rules?"

He laughed. "Of course I do. My parents love the beach. I practically grew up playing."

I relaxed. Perhaps my personal bodyguard wasn't still right

by my side, but I wasn't alone. Jackson seemed like a good guy and at least Thad hadn't tried to join us.

Jackson's eyes met mine, and they twinkled in the sunlight. "I'm happy to help if you need it."

"Thanks." I blushed. Was he flirting or just being nice?

Chris served the ball and Jackson returned it. The game continued seamlessly.

Half an hour later, Alec hadn't returned yet. The breeze picked up, and the temperature dropped a few degrees. We finished the game and decided to pack up. There would be plenty of time to play in nicer weather.

I scanned the area, not wanting to leave without Alec, but I wasn't sure where he'd gotten to. I didn't have my phone so I couldn't send him a message to ask.

The wind whipped briskly across my bare skin and I shivered.

"Here." Jackson, who'd been helping put the volleyball gear away, offered me his sweater.

I waved dismissively. "Thanks, but I'll be fine."

He raised his eyebrows. "I can see your goose bumps from here. I'm not cold. My hairy arms have more insulation than yours. Just take it and give it back to me later."

I hesitated, but then said, "Thank you."

It wasn't a big deal. Accepting his sweater didn't mean what it would have in high school. He was just being nice.

I took it from him and was about to put it on when Alec appeared from behind one of the palm trees near the path leading deeper into the resort. He marched over, tore the sweater from my grasp and thrust it back into Jackson's hands.

"Thanks, but I've got her covered," he growled, his eyes flashing. He unwrapped one of his team jerseys from around his waist and gestured for me to hold my arms out so he could put it on me. I did, feeling a little like an exhibit at a zoo. What the hell was going on?

The soft fabric enveloped me and stopped the worst of the chill from the wind. When I poked my head through the head hole and blinked against the sun, I noticed that Jackson was gone.

"What are you doing?" I asked Alec, completely baffled.

He put his hands on my hips and, despite the layer of fabric separating us, it felt painfully intimate. "If you were really my girl, I'd never let you wear another man's clothing. The only name on your jersey should be mine."

TWELVE

ALEC

The dying light of the sun painted the sky shades of pink and orange as Tally and I sipped our drinks on lounge chairs near the pool. Quiet music played in the background and it would have been wonderfully peaceful, if not for the rapidly approaching figure of Lake.

I studied her, wondering if we could get out of there before she arrived and avoid whatever it was she wanted to talk about because the briskness of her stride and the determined angle of her chin said that she had some kind of agenda. I'd been enjoying my after dinner soda while Tally indulged in a cocktail. I couldn't be bothered to deal with an interruption, especially not an unwelcome one.

"Incoming." I tilted my head toward Lake.

Tally followed the movement and grimaced. She and Lake had seemed to be getting along well enough during our game of beach volleyball earlier, but I supposed being in a group setting was different from having a direct conversation, which obviously wasn't something she wanted.

"We could run," I suggested, only half-teasing.

"It will be fine." It sounded like she was willing herself to believe it. "Lake is a nice person."

"Just not the most self-aware," I added and sipped my soda. Both sisters were like that.

Lake came to a stop in front of us and steepled her hands together. "Okay. I have to be quick because Chris and I are due for a romantic spa date soon, but I needed to catch you before tomorrow."

Tally pushed her sunglasses up her nose and angled her head back to get a better look at her. "What's up?"

Lake hesitated, but then jumped in. "Look, this is awkward, and I'm sorry to ask, but could you two just lay off the happy couple thing for a bit?"

I stared at her, stunned. I'd had no idea what she was going to say, but this sure as hell hadn't factored in as an option. I reached across and took Tally's hand to show my support. Lake's comment didn't hurt me, but Tally could definitely take it the wrong way. Honestly, I wasn't sure there was a right way to take it.

Lake motioned toward our joined hands. "See, that's what I mean."

"I don't understand," Tally said.

A few different emotions flitted across Lake's face, but I definitely caught a glimpse of anxiety and perhaps a hint of guilt. My metaphorical hackles rose, and I clasped Tally's hand tighter.

Lake sighed and looked around, perhaps searching for another chair, but when she didn't see any, she remained standing. "Coral is upset by the tension between you and Thad. It would really help things go smoothly if you would stop rubbing your new relationship in Thad's face."

"Excuse me?" Tally demanded, whipping off her sunglasses.

"Especially when it's clear to everyone that he isn't the only one that cheated," Lake continued, as if she didn't realize how deeply she'd just ventured into the danger zone.

Fury simmered in my gut as I straightened. "You have some nerve saying that."

"Why?" She flipped her hair back. "It's true. People don't move on this quickly, and you guys have known each other forever; you've probably been sneaking around with each other for years too."

I drew in a deep breath, ready to blast her with a list of all the ways in which she was completely wrong, but Tally squeezed my hand in warning and I caught myself. I wanted to chew Lake out, but I needed to remember a few things.

This was her wedding, and Coral was her sister. Of course she wanted the event to go smoothly and for her sister to be happy. She was just going about making it happen in a really shitty way.

"I never cheated on Thad," Tally said levelly.

"Here's what actually happened," I added, "in case you're interested in the truth instead of rumors."

Lake had the decency to blush.

"Tally called me, in tears because she'd found Coral and Thad in bed together when she went home early to surprise him. I picked her up, took her home, and did my best to comfort her. As you can imagine, she was pretty fucking upset."

"Of course," Lake murmured.

"Her confidence was knocked, and I made it my mission to repair it. During that time, we got closer than ever and things shifted. Became more. She was faithful to that asshole, even though he didn't deserve it." I paused, considered how much more to say, decided to go for it. "This may be your wedding, but I won't tolerate anyone being rude to Tally."

Tally tried to shush me, but I ignored her.

"She's done nothing wrong." My voice was steely. "She deserves better."

Lake's eyes darted between us and she gnawed on her lower lip. "This really didn't start before the breakup?"

Tally shook her head. "It really didn't."

Lake deflated slowly, like a leaky balloon. "I'm sorry. It seemed obvious that that's what must have happened. I didn't mean to hurt anyone."

"It's fine," Tally said.

I wanted to argue. It wasn't fine. But I'd said my part, so I kept my mouth shut.

"I'm sorry if me being here has caused problems for you," Tally continued, and that time, I couldn't keep quiet. I started to talk, but to my surprise, Lake beat me to the punch.

"Don't be ridiculous." Lake waved dismissively. "Alec is right. You're not the one who fucked up. Just... Ugh. Do you think you could consider what I said? Maybe try to get along with Thad? I know it's not easy, but it would be really nice if I could, you know, enjoy my wedding without any drama."

"We'll try," Tally promised.

"Great." Lake backed off. "I have a date to get to. Don't get too drunk!"

She spun around and sashayed away.

As soon as she was out of sight, Tally drained the rest of her cocktail.

"Do you mind if we go back to our room?" she asked.

"Not at all." I stood and pulled her with me. Her palm was warm and soft against my larger, rougher one. I expected her to let go as we started walking toward the main resort building, but instead, her fingers remained linked with mine.

"You don't have to come with me," she said, glancing toward me, her expression strained. "I don't feel in the mood to be social tonight, so I'd understand if you'd rather explore the resort and see who else is around."

I smiled. "I'd rather be with you."

Her nose scrunched. "Sorry for being a killjoy."

"Don't be. Like I said, none of this is your fault." I'd repeat it however many times were needed before the message sunk in.

In the lobby, we passed Jackson and Ben, and I couldn't help the smug curl of my lips as Jackson's gaze lowered to our joined hands. Still, he gave a friendly dip of his head as we entered the elevator, swiped a card, and pushed the button for our floor.

I checked the time. "There might be a hockey game on."

The elevator doors opened and we made for our room.

Tally propped her sunglasses on the top of her head. "I think the Chaos were playing tonight Do you think we could find a replay?"

"I'll check." I unlocked our door and held it open while Tally entered. She switched on the TV and I grabbed the remote and scrolled through channels until I found one with a hockey game underway. Sure enough, the Chicago Chaos were playing Washington.

I watched as Austin Harris, the team's best scorer and my younger sister's boss, glided up the center of the ice toward the goal, the puck on the end of his stick. He tried to flick it past the goalie but it hit the goalie's glove and deflected. The defense were on it immediately, sending the puck back toward the other end of the ice.

Tally flopped onto the bed and sighed. "They're not having a good season."

"Do they ever?"

The team might have some decent players, like Harrison and his fellow first line forward Nick Kelly, but there was absolutely no cohesion. They were like a bunch of strangers forced together. Or worse, colleagues who actively disliked each other forced into a team bonding activity.

I lay down alongside Tally, propping myself up on the stack of pillows so I could watch the game. One of the men in the Chaos's distinctive blue and silver uniform yanked his gloves off and rounded on an opposing player.

"There goes Taggert," I said.

Tally snorted. "I'll never understand why they made him captain. He has too much of a temper."

She wasn't wrong. Taggert was a mean player, and he lost his shit easily.

"Could be worse though," I pointed out. "McKinley is a complete loose cannon."

She nodded. "But he's in the second line and only a couple of years into the league. Taggert is a veteran. He should know better."

Warmth bloomed inside me. Fuck, I loved that Tally and I could talk hockey together.

"I still can't believe that Jane is working for Harris after that big song and dance about making her own way," I said.

Because of our father and uncle playing in the NHL, Jane and I had been raised in the public eye, but while it had never bothered me too much—beyond teaching me to watch what I said and did—Jane had hated it.

She'd turned down our parents' offer to pay for her to attend a nearby university, instead opting to move to Chicago and support herself by working as a personal assistant. I didn't understand her need to put distance between us or her insistence on not letting Mom and Dad make life easier for her when they were desperate to help. I respected her need for independence though, even if I didn't fully agree with her choices.

Tally's head moved closer to mine and I found myself subconsciously angling my body toward hers. She shuffled over and rested her cheek on my shoulder. I wrapped my arm around her and breathed in the fruity scent of her shampoo combined with a lingering saltiness from the ocean breeze.

We watched Washington decimate the Chaos. Taggert threw more fists. Harris was blocked from scoring another three times. While Taggert was in the penalty box, his replacement, McKinley, went ballistic and had to be pulled off one of Washington's wingers by his own teammates.

It was a mess, but entertaining as hell.

When the final whistle blew, I looked down at Tally. Her eyelashes fanned over her cheeks, her lips were slightly parted, and her chest rose and fell gently. I chuckled. Somehow, she'd managed to fall asleep.

I maneuvered her off me and gazed at her for a long moment. Damn, she was stunning. Pink cheeks, plump lips, generous curves.

My cock filled as I imagined how it would feel to slide it between those lips. I shook my head, trying to dispel the misplaced surge of attraction, but it was too late. I was already hard.

Shit.

I looked around the room. I could roll over and ignore it, the way I had last night, but I was even more pent up now than I had been then, and I needed to get some sleep. If I was over-tired, my training would suffer. I wasn't exactly a veteran of the sport, but I wasn't one of the younger players on the team either. I needed every advantage I could get.

I'd just have to take care of it.

Decision made, I slid slowly off the bed so as not to wake

Tally and padded softly to the bathroom. I locked the door, lowered my shorts and underwear, and took myself in hand.

I pumped briskly, eager to get this over with. If I took my time, I might be tempted to fantasize or to draw out my pleasure. I needed this to be mechanical. Simply fulfilling my body's needs without any fanfare.

My breathing grew ragged and my balls drew up. I pressed my lips together and forced myself to breathe through my nose, so the noise wouldn't be loud enough to disturb Tally.

My cock pulsed in my palm, hot and heavy, so close to the edge. A few more strokes, a twist of the wrist, and I came, an image of Tally's glossy pink lips flashing through my mind.

Fuck.

THIRTEEN

TALLY

The sky overhead was gray as I picked my way along the sand in bare feet, listening to the footsteps behind me coming nearer. I hadn't looked to see who it was. Hopefully just a resort guest, although knowing my luck, that was unlikely.

I gazed over the water. It was farther out at the moment, lines in the sand showing where the tide had been earlier. While the clouds had gathered and the breeze was enough that I'd had to wear a sweater, the sea itself was flat. It hardly moved except for the rhythmic hiss of water over sand as waves lapped at the beach.

The footsteps behind me slapped against the wet ground. Whoever was coming made no effort to preserve the peacefulness of the morning.

"Tally."

I stiffened, recognizing the voice immediately. Seriously, couldn't he leave me alone for just half a day?

I considered ignoring him but knew he wouldn't give up until he'd achieved whatever it was he wanted.

"What?" I asked, turning to face Thad.

My ex looked exhausted, with dark circles beneath his eyes and brackets around his mouth that made him seem older than he was.

Perhaps he wasn't sleeping well. Or maybe Coral had had a crisis of conscience and kicked him out, although that seemed like too much to hope for.

"What's going on with you?" he demanded, his flip flops slapping as he crossed the final distance between us and stopped a few feet away. "I thought you'd be upset about me and Coral, but you're acting like you never cared about me."

I stared at him, my jaw slack. "Did you...*want* me to care?"

For a moment, he flushed as though embarrassed, but then his upper lip curled in a sneer. "I just want to know if I never mattered to you because you're sure as hell making it seem that way."

"What do you want me to say?" I demanded, picking my jaw up, stunned by his audacity. "Did you come here hoping to see me crying in a corner about my broken heart while you parade around with my cousin?"

His lips moved but no sound came out.

I took a step forward. "Did you want me to be hurting? Is that what this is? You feel robbed because I'm not as devastated as you'd like me to be?"

"O-of course not," he stammered, looking taken aback. "I'm not the bad guy here. You always said that you and Alec were just friends, but apparently, you're screwing him now. What the hell is going on?"

I raised my chin. "It's none of your business what's happening between Alec and me. You and I aren't together anymore, so you get no say in the matter."

He scoffed. "It sure as fuck is my business if you were sleeping around on me."

My chest tightened. I tried to suck in a breath, but it got caught in my throat.

"How—" The word squeezed out but cut off too quickly. I inhaled roughly and tried again. "How dare you accuse me of that?"

First Lake and now Thad. Was that really what everyone thought of me? That I was a cheater?

"I'm the one who had to go to the clinic to get tested for STDs," I hissed, leaning close so that no one else on the nearly empty beach would be able to overhear us. "I'm the one who had to explain to a nurse that my boyfriend had proven he couldn't be trusted. I had to wait days for the results. Do you know how stressful that is?"

Thad rolled his eyes. "As if I'd ever risk going without a condom."

"How would I know what you'd risk?" I shrieked, clamping my hands firmly to my hips because, otherwise, I might lose control and slap him across the face. "I didn't think you'd have sex with my cousin, but you did. I don't know you at all!"

We both fell silent except for the sound of my ragged breathing. We stared at each other, neither of us seeming to know what to say.

A figure moved behind Thad. I blinked and squinted as they came into focus.

It was Alec.

Chunks of wet sand sprayed everywhere as he pounded along the beach toward us, heedless of his surroundings. He kept a wide berth around Thad, slung his arm around my shoulder and drew me tightly against him. His glare was locked on Thad, and even as he kissed my temple, his focus on my ex didn't waver.

"Leave her the fuck alone." Alec practically vibrated with

rage. "Can't you see you've upset her? Haven't you done enough?"

Thad's nostrils flared. "I deserve to know what my girlfriend was doing while we were together."

I grimaced. Perhaps I'd been getting through to him, but any progress I'd made was shot to hell now.

"I never cheated on you," I said tiredly.

"You've got your answer." Alec steered me away from him. "Come on, cocobug. Your Dad was just telling me about a bakery down the road that they visited yesterday. Let's go and check it out."

He didn't pull away as we started to walk, and his proximity warmed me inside.

"That sounds nice," I said, allowing him to put distance between us and Thad.

With his free hand, he took his phone from his pocket and opened a maps app. He guided us through the resort and out onto the road. A paved sidewalk stretched alongside it, and after only a few minutes, we arrived at a small cluster of shops.

The bakery was immediately obvious because of the small, square tables with white and blue sun umbrellas arranged outside. Alec opened the door and held it for me as I entered. The interior was just as cute, with comfy-looking chairs in the same shades of blue and white as the umbrellas.

Alec led me to the display cabinet and my mouth watered at the delicious array of pastries, cakes, and bread. I chose a glossy chocolate croissant with pastry that looked buttery and flaky and had chocolate oozing from within.

Alec ordered a prosciutto and mozzarella sandwich, as well as a coffee for each of us, then we took a number and retreated to one of the tables nearest the floor-to-ceiling windows looking out onto the street. A slatted wood wall separated us from the next table over and we were out of sight of the main entrance.

It didn't take long for our food to arrive, along with a plain black coffee for Alec and a caramel macchiato for me. I stirred my coffee and tasted it.

Mm. The perfect mix of sweet and dark.

Next, I tried the croissant. The pastry melted on my tongue. I closed my eyes and moaned. When I opened them again, Alec was staring at me.

"What?" I asked, self-conscious. "Is there something on my face?"

"No." He blew a breath out of the corner of his mouth. "I just can't look away from your lips."

My pulse thrummed faster and my tongue darted out to dampen my lips. Suddenly, I was more aware of them than I'd ever been in my life.

What was I supposed to say to that?

My fork clanged against the plate and I set it down, my hands trembling too badly for me to use it.

Alec's dark gaze continued to burn into mine. "Ever since we kissed that first night here, I can't stop thinking of you. You're so sexy, Tally, but you're more than that. You're sweet and smart and more kind than most people deserve, but you don't let people walk all over you either."

I hid my hands beneath the table, resting them on my thighs. All words had deserted me and I just had to hope that Alec was happy to maintain a one-sided conversation.

"I think..." He swallowed, his throat bobbling. "I don't want to pretend anymore. I want to be with you for real."

I tugged at the bottom of my ear lobe, as if doing so might change the words I was hearing. I drew in a slow breath and looked down at my croissant, the chocolate forming a mess on the plate that now appealed about as much as eating ash.

In a way, Alec was voicing a dream I'd never dared to hope for, but being faced with the possibility of my fantasy becoming real was scarier than I ever could have imagined. What if he was just being impulsive and changed his mind when he realized he wasn't actually interested in me romantically?

"Are you sure?" I asked cautiously.

"What do you mean?" He almost sounded offended.

I rubbed my lips together, hoping he wouldn't take this the wrong way. "We kissed, and it was nice."

"Nice?" His eyes narrowed. "It was incredible."

"Okay," I allowed. "It was incredible. But it's been a long time since you had sex—unless you're keeping things from me—so maybe that's all you really want? It would make sense if you're lonely and latched onto me because I'm here and familiar and comfortable."

A groove formed between Alec's eyebrows. "Did you just try to mansplain my feelings to me?"

I opened my mouth, a protest on my tongue, but then snapped it shut.

Well, damn. I guess I had.

"I'm sorry," I said weakly.

He nodded, as if this was his due. "I know how I feel, Tally. I've had blue balls plenty of times before. That's not what this is. It's taken a while to get my head around it, but the truth is, I want you, and not just for a fling. When I look into the future, the only person I can imagine sharing it with is you."

My heart thumped erratically. "Me?"

"Yeah." He offered me a tentative smile. "You're my person. Who else would I want?"

I hesitated, desperate to leap on his offer before he changed his mind, but the very fact I worried he might decide he didn't want me after all was enough to make me pause.

I pushed my plate aside. "We've been really good friends, but we can't be sure there's enough chemistry between us for our relationship to be more than that."

What would happen if we tried it, realized we weren't physically compatible for some reason, and ruined our friendship in the process?

I couldn't lose him. He meant too much to me.

Alec snorted. "After that kiss we shared, there's no way you can doubt our chemistry. It was hot."

Desire heated my core at the memory. The spark between us really had been brilliant.

"I don't want to push you," he continued, his tone gentling. "Especially not when you only just got out of a relationship and you're still hurting from his betrayal."

"I can't lie and say it hasn't made me more hesitant."

His gaze turned sad. "I know, baby. But I'll never hurt you like that, and I'm prepared to wait for as long as it takes if you think there's even a chance that we could have a happy relationship."

I searched my mind for an answer, but it was frustratingly blank. I wanted to say yes, but was that the smart decision? I was so twisted in knots that I couldn't tell.

"Don't rush," he said, but there was a flicker of hurt in his eyes, and I knew he must have hoped that I'd be more excited to jump into a relationship than this.

Guilt twisted my gut. I didn't want to hurt him. And honestly, I did want to be with him. I was just afraid to make that jump, and I didn't know what to say to make him understand me without causing him pain or doubt.

"I... uh..."

FOURTEEN

TALLY

My heart was going crazy, battering against my ribs like it wanted to beat out of my chest. My throat felt tight and my head spun.

I was terrified of losing Alec.

If we started a relationship and it didn't work out, that could spell the end of our friendship. But things had changed anyway. We'd kissed and shared a bed, and he'd told me he had feelings for me.

There was no going back.

Whatever happened, our relationship would be irrevocably changed. Now, it was just up to me to decide what shape I wanted that change to take.

I scraped my teeth over my lip and wiped my hands on my shorts. "You're certain there's enough chemistry between us for something real? Something that could last?"

He nodded. "Not a doubt in my mind."

"Then prove it."

With a glance at my croissant, he asked, "Are you going to finish that?"

I sighed. At this point there was no chance in hell. I'd have to come back and get another one when I regained my appetite. "No, I'm done."

He stood and rounded the table, holding his hand out to me. I placed my hand on his and let him pull me to my feet. Hand-in-hand, we circled the slatted wall. A stranger to our left buried their face in a newspaper but neither of us looked at them as we made our way out of the bakery.

"What are we doing?" I asked as Alec led me down the street toward the resort.

He smirked, and the expression had a flirty edge to it. "I am proving to you that we have plenty of chemistry."

"How?"

"With a kiss, if you'll let me. Maybe more, depending on what you're comfortable with." He stopped, and turned to face me. "Seriously, Tally, your comfort is the most important thing to me, so if you're not ready for anything at all right now, then we can just lie side-by-side on the bed and talk."

I swallowed, imagining how it might feel to release control of the sparks of electricity I'd sensed between us during our "pretend" kiss.

"I'd like a kiss," I admitted.

"Then we'll start with that and go from there," he said, giving my hand a gentle squeeze and continuing along the sidewalk.

At the resort, we skirted around the edge of the lobby, eager to avoid anyone we might know, and went straight to the elevator. We managed to get to our room without running into any acquaintances. Alec's hands were irritatingly steady as he unlocked our door.

Inside, it suddenly struck me that I was about to kiss my

best friend. This time, it wouldn't come out of nowhere. I would be expecting it. And somehow, that made it all the more terrifying.

A little exhilarating too.

"Are you sure about this?" Alec asked, letting go of my hand and putting a few feet of distance between us.

"Yes."

Really, what choice did I have? Things were going to change between us regardless of what decision we made now. I'd rather take the chance that we might, maybe, be able to have a wonderful new relationship together than hold back out of fear and lose him completely.

He put his hands on my hips and backed me against the wall. His big, strong body caged me in and the wall prevented me from escaping the sensual gravity of his presence.

Slowly, without hesitation, he lowered his head toward mine. Unable to resist the anticipation, I stretched onto my toes and touched my lips to his.

The kiss was gentle, soft, but then a deep growl rumbled in his throat, and he pinned me more forcefully against the wall. I parted my lips, and he deepened the kiss, sweeping his tongue inside and stealing my ability to think rationally.

I closed my eyes and breathed in citrus and a trace of clean, masculine sweat. He cupped my face, tilting my head back to give himself better access to my mouth. I plastered myself against him, whimpering at the delicious friction between our bodies.

My nipples rubbed his hard chest and desire skittered down my spine and pooled in my pelvis. He ground into me. I could feel the hard bulge of his cock where it pressed against my pussy.

Then, all of a sudden, he tore away from me. His mouth hung open, his breath coming in ragged gasps. His eyes stared into mine, his pupils blown out, black bleeding into the brown of his irises.

"I think we have chemistry," he said. "Don't you?"

I blinked at him, momentarily uncertain what he was talking about until I recalled our earlier conversation. A giggle burst from me, unbidden. "Maybe just a little."

He drew in a slow, steady breath, visibly trying to calm himself. Against my will, I found my gaze drawn to the tented front of his shorts.

"So, shall we lie down and talk?" he asked.

For a few seconds, I didn't think he was serious, but his expression didn't waver. He was really willing to stop right now if I wasn't interested in going further.

My heart warmed. I'd always known Alec was a good guy, always wondered how on earth he was single, and now he was proving that I hadn't been wrong to think that way.

My tongue darted out, tasting a little of his coffee on my lips. "What if I feel like doing something else?"

Impossibly, his eyes darkened further. "Like what?"

"Like...seeing where all of this chemistry goes."

Even from a kiss, I knew that we could be combustible together. I wanted to experience that, and I wanted it now.

He shifted slightly closer. "What do you want, cocobug? I need you to say it. Do you want my tongue on your sweet little pussy? Do you want my cock deep inside you? Tell me, and I'll give it to you."

My pussy throbbed in response to his hot words.

I bit my lower lip and my cheeks heated. I wasn't ashamed of my sexual appetite, but I wasn't usually much of a dirty talker either.

"I want you to make me come," I told him, knowing that my face must be a furious shade of scarlet.

His nostrils flared, and he grabbed me by the hips. "Done. Do you have any limits?"

"No. I trust you."

He paused, his dark eyes locked on mine. "I won't let you down."

He grabbed my waistband and peeled the layer off, baring me except for a pair of pink panties. He knelt and, before I had time to feel self-conscious, he buried his face in the vee of my thighs. Heat blasted through me.

I stared down at his dark hair, stunned. He mouthed me through my panties, stimulating my clit, providing the sexiest sight of my life.

His fingers hooked in the sides of my panties, and he edged them down, bit by bit, revealing more of me until my lower half was nude in front of him.

"God, this is the prettiest pussy I've ever seen."

His tongue delved between my thighs, licking down my center, driving me crazy in the best way.

Suddenly, he rose to his feet and swept me into his arms, lifting me clean off the floor.

I gasped and clutched at him. "What are you doing?"

None of my lovers had ever lifted me before. That said, none had been as muscular as Alec either. He deposited me on the bed, lowered himself between my thighs, and got to work erasing my memories of any other men who'd gone down on me.

It was like my pleasure turned him on. Any time he licked or touched me in a way I liked, he seemed to know and doubled down.

My thoughts grew fuzzy, my mind pleasantly hazy. All of my senses were consumed by him. The sight of his gorgeous face each time he raised it to meet my eyes, the smell of sex in the air, the sound of his tongue in my wetness, and the vibrations of his groans against my tender flesh.

He wound me tighter and tighter, then slipped a finger inside and crooked it slightly. His thumb teased my clit in gentle circles and my hips arched off the bed. If he kept this up, I was going to come without him even being inside me, and that wouldn't do.

I needed him in me. Now.

"Do you have a condom?" I asked breathlessly, praying the answer was yes. I'd packed one, but it pre-dated Thad because he'd always insisted on providing his own, so I wasn't sure what kind of condition it was in.

"Yeah." He reared back and scanned my face. "You sure? There's no rush. I can get you off like this."

"I want it. But only if you do."

"I've never wanted anything more." He tugged the hem of my shirt. "Take this off."

While he scrambled to find a condom in his wallet and rapidly shed his clothes, I sat up and drew my shirt over my head. I unclipped my bra and tossed it aside, watching Alec's features carefully for any sign that he might not like what he saw.

His jaw tightened and he approached me, the forgotten foil-wrapped condom dangling from between his fingers.

"Your tits are fucking gorgeous." He dropped the condom on the bed and cupped a hand around each of my breasts, cradling them in his callused palms. His thumbs brushed my nipples and his breath caught. "So soft and pink."

He dropped to his belly and planted his face between them, inhaling deeply, then he used the tip of his tongue to tease my nipples into stiff peaks. I threw my head back and clutched the covers. My nipples had never seemed particularly sensitive before, but apparently, the other guys had just been doing it wrong.

Alec was most definitely doing it right.

He got lost in my body, playing with me like I was his favorite toy until I was panting and desperate for him to fill me.

"Please," I begged. "Don't make me wait any longer."

He blinked, the glassiness clearing from his eyes. "Sorry, cocobug. I've got you."

He slid the condom on and pushed inside me easily. My body wanted him so badly that there was no discomfort, only the exquisite pleasure of having him closer to me than he'd ever been before.

I cried out, and his mouth latched onto my throat and sucked until I swatted at him. "No hickies!"

He grunted. "I want everyone to know you're mine."

"They do." As if anyone could think anything else after the show we'd put on over the last few days.

"They'd better."

His lips found mine and we kissed as he began to thrust inside me.

"Fuck," he muttered against my mouth. "You feel so good. So hot and tight. You're close to coming already, aren't you?"

"Yes, damn you." I stood no chance against him when he seemed so consumed by every part of me.

He tilted his hips in just such a way that every one of his movements caused friction against my clit. First, just light brushes, then harder and firmer until my orgasm rolled through me and I shuddered and called out his name.

"That's it, cocobug. Good girl."

He plunged into me over and over until his thrusts became jerky. His cock pulsed and he came inside me.

He rolled off me, disposed of the condom, and pulled me into an embrace. His lips caressed my temple.

"What do you think?" he asked quietly. "Am I boyfriend material?"

My stomach lurched.

"You are," I admitted. "But I'm scared to lose you."

He rolled onto his side and turned to face me. His hand rested on my hip and he smiled at me like I was every good thing that had ever happened to him.

"I'm scared too, but you're worth the risk. Tally, you're worth *everything*."

I kissed the curve of his smile. "Then let's risk it all."

FIFTEEN

TALLY

I lay in bed, flat on my back, debating for the fiftieth time whether I should wake Alec up with kisses.

I wanted to. God, it was tempting, but after we'd holed up in our room yesterday and spent the whole time exploring each other in new ways—in between breaks for room service—I could use a little time to think.

Yesterday, we'd been flying high on positive emotions and sex hormones. Now, in the quiet hours of the morning, my mind was clearer and I'd be better able to figure out where to go from here.

I lifted Alec's arm, which he'd draped across my belly, and slowly eased out from under it. I slipped one leg off the edge of the bed and then the other. I inched away from him, wary of shifting too much of my weight at once and alerting him to the fact I'd woken.

If he stirred now, he'd probably kiss me and drag me into another round of lovemaking. I wasn't opposed to that, exactly, but it would addle my mind for another few hours, and then I'd have missed my window for contemplation.

Little by little, I eased onto my feet. I'd love a shower because I must smell like sex, but the water would disturb Alec. Best to just get changed and leave. I could shower later.

I found a pair of yoga pants on the floor near my suitcase, grabbed it, and quietly opened the suitcase and rifled through until I'd found underwear and a tank top. I dressed and let myself out of the hotel room.

I made my way down to the beach, pausing by the outdoor activities shed to collect a yoga mat, which I tucked under my arm and took with me onto the sand. A handful of people were out and about. More than I'd expected, but it was the warmest morning of our stay, the air almost unpleasantly humid and without much wind, so it made sense that guests would want to paddle in the shallows to cool off.

I walked a couple hundred yards along the beach, unrolled the yoga mat, and positioned it so that I could watch the waves as I did my sun salutations. I started in mountain pose, transitioned to a forward fold, to downward dog, plank, up-dog, back to downward dog, and returned to mountain in a series of fluid movements.

I cycled through the short set of poses six times before moving into the body of my yoga practice. Warrior two pose came first, then sun warrior, extended warrior, and a repeated shift back and forth between the three, stretching one side and then the other.

As I brought my legs back to the center and took my weight onto my left foot, I wondered what the change in my relationship with Alec would mean in the wider context of our lives. Our friendship was irrevocably altered, no matter what happened. However much it worried me, I'd accepted that.

But what would it mean for me to have a boyfriend in the NHL?

Waves lapped at the sand, and I extended my arms ahead of me, preparing to enter warrior three.

I already went to all of Alec's home games, and I knew many of the other players' partners didn't attend away games, so it wasn't like I'd be expected to do that. Just as well, since I was so busy with Coco Luxe.

Would the media care more about who I was now that I was dating Alec? They'd never bothered me much before, but we hadn't hid the fact we were old school friends and it wasn't a particularly exciting story, so they'd left me alone. But if we were old-friends-turned-happy-couple, that might be an angle worth investigating. The public adored a good love story.

Would they disrupt Coco Luxe?

I gently placed my foot on the ground and transferred my weight to the other foot, extending my left leg out behind me and circling my arms forward. A gull screeched overhead.

No, I couldn't see any potential increased media interest in me being a negative thing for Coco Luxe. If anything, it might be good for the business.

As another upside, Alec worked at least as many hours as me, if not more. Combined with travel, it meant he wouldn't hound me to focus less on my business, like Thad had. Unfortunately, it also meant less time with him, but it wouldn't be forever. The length of a professional sportsman's career was limited.

One of the major downsides was that I'd have to live with the knowledge that women would likely throw themselves at him every time he was out of town. I trusted that he wouldn't cheat on me. Alec was a good man. He'd never hurt anyone the way Thad had done to me, but it would be irritating to know how many people wished they could steal him from me.

I returned to a standing position and shook out my feet, then pressed the bottom of my right foot into the inside of my left thigh and put my palms together in front of my chest.

Closing my eyes, I allowed myself to become aware of the world behind me, using my other senses. The air was warm as it passed through my nose, and it carried the scent of seawater. A little girl laughed farther down the beach, and nearby, someone's feet kicked up sand as they drew closer.

Frowning, I opened my eyes and looked around.

Coral smiled at me tentatively and tucked her loose hair behind her ear. "Can we talk?"

I lowered my foot to the mat. "I suppose so."

It wouldn't do me any good to avoid her forever. Especially now that I was genuinely with Alec and couldn't care less about Thad—except for my wounded pride.

I sat cross-legged on the mat and she dropped onto the sand opposite me and mirrored my position.

For an uncomfortably long time, she gazed at me. In a lot of ways, it was like staring into a mirror. Our eyes were so similar.

In other ways, we were completely different. My hair was dark, hers was light. I was curvy, she was slim. I was pale, she was golden.

"I'm sorry about Thad." The words fell from her lips on a gust of air, as if the apology had deflated her. "It was horrible of me to...to...sleep with him while you were together. You and I have always gotten along well and I hate being at odds like this. Especially when it's my fault. I... I don't know; I think I was so flattered by his attention that what we were doing felt naughty rather than just wrong."

I stayed quiet. I didn't particularly feel like accepting her apology, or her excuses, but dragging it out wouldn't help anything either. Whatever happened, we'd always be family. There was no getting away from that. At some point, we'd have to bury the hatchet. Well, either that or I could become bitter for the rest of my life.

"Anyway," she carried on, fidgeting with her hands, obviously nervous. "It just kind of happened, and after it did, I figured the damage was done, right? So it didn't matter if I did it again."

I supposed that answered the question as to whether it had been a one-time thing or an ongoing affair.

"How exactly did it 'just happen?'" I asked, because honestly, that sounded a bit weak. "Did you magically find yourself inside his apartment? Did your clothes accidentally vanish? Did his dick just fall into your pussy?"

Her chin wobbled, but she held it high, accepting my snarky comments as her due. "We met at a bar one night. I was a bit drunk. He invited me back to his place to sober up, and it all spiraled out of control."

"I see." In a way, it was good to know the details, but I'd also be happy to never speak of the matter again.

"I swear, I never meant to hurt you." Tears gleamed in her eyes. "I'm so ashamed of myself. I don't like the person I've been lately, and I'm sorry about what an asshole Thad has been since we got here. I don't know what his problem is, but I told him to pack his bags and leave. He won't bother you anymore."

I released a stuttered breath. "Thank you."

She wriggled closer and glanced at my hands as if debating whether to reach for them but then opted not to. "I want to fix this. And for us to get along again. What can I do?"

The corner of my eye twitched. She looked so miserable and her apology seemed genuine, but it was all still too raw.

"I appreciate your apology." I spoke softly, hoping that would cushion the blow. "And it's nice that you want to try to make it up to me, but I'm not there yet. I never expected you to betray me like this and I need more time to be in an emotional place where I'm ready to forgive you. I'll get there. Just, not yet."

Tears welled in Coral's eyes and spilled down her cheeks.

"I'm sorry," she sobbed. "I'm a horrible person. I'm so sorry."

I grimaced, uncertain what to do. She'd hurt me, so I didn't feel like comforting her, but she also seemed to be doing a pretty good job of beating herself up, and I didn't want to add to the load.

"It's not all bad," I said eventually.

She looked up at me, crying silently now. "It's not?"

I shrugged. "At least I know that Thad wasn't the right person for me. If not for this, I might not have gotten together with Alec, and I'm pretty happy with how that worked out."

The side of her mouth hitched up in the tiniest trace of a smile.

I started to smile back, but then I caught sight of the six-foot-plus man storming down the beach behind her, and my smile vanished.

Alec looked ready to rain fire and brimstone over the landscape.

Oh, shit.

SIXTEEN

ALEC

"What's going on?" I demanded as I reached Tally and Coral.

I'd been disappointed upon waking alone. I'd wanted to make love to my new girlfriend. Based on the fact she was sitting there with a yoga mat, she'd come out to exercise and think, and that lessened my irritation. I could understand the need for space to work things through. What I didn't understand was the cheating bitch keeping her company.

Tally met my gaze. Her eyes were dry and she didn't seem upset, which was something, at least. "Coral is apologizing."

I narrowed my eyes at Coral. I could tell she was doing her best to appear adorable and harmless. Too bad for her I wasn't like Thad; a pair of sad eyes did nothing for me if they were set in any face that didn't belong to Tally.

"Just leave us alone." I crossed my arms. "You've done enough to hurt Tally already. Surely it isn't too much to ask for you to have the decency to keep your distance."

Splotches of red blossomed on Coral's face and she staggered to her feet and hurried away without another word.

"You didn't have to be that rude." Tally pushed herself upright and dusted sand off her hands. "Yes, I'm angry, and yes, she hurt me, but at least she's trying to mend bridges."

I stared at her, unable to believe what I was hearing. "There's no fixing this. She fucked up, and now she has to live with it."

Something regretful flashed in Tally's eyes and she sighed. "I know, but it's nice that she cares, even if it's too little too late."

"Just don't let her walk all over you." I unfolded my arms, leaned over and kissed her cheek. "Now, do you mind telling me why you weren't in my bed when I woke up?"

She studied her bare feet, which suddenly seemed to fascinate her. "I had to clear my mind."

Even though I'd realized this, a hint of panic clawed at my insides.

"Are you having second thoughts?" I asked.

"What?" Her startled gaze met mine. "No. But everything happened so fast yesterday, and it was good—really good—but a little overwhelming."

The clawing panic receded. I took her hand, raised it to my lips, and kissed the back of it.

"You still want to be with me?" I needed to hear the words.

"Yes." She smiled and wrapped her arms around my waist. "You make me happy."

My heart skipped. "You make me happy too, cocobug." I kissed her forehead. "Now, do you want to finish your routine?"

I'd happily sit and watch her or jog down the beach until she was done.

She shook her head. "No. I needed a little clarity, and I got it. Would you like some breakfast?"

"That sounds great."

Kneeling, she rolled up the yoga mat and tucked it under her arm. "Come on then. I'll get rid of this and we can visit the buffet."

We started along the beach together. Birds cheeped from the trees and the waves whispered over the sand. The air was warm but not hot enough to be unpleasant, and the clear sky indicated it was going to be a beautiful day.

I reclaimed her free hand and intertwined our fingers. The wind stirred her hair, carrying the familiar scent of fruit—along with a hint of sex—toward me.

I couldn't have asked for a more perfect moment.

If I'd ever harbored even a sliver of doubt that Tally was the woman for me, it vanished as we strolled side-by-side along the sand and onto the path to the resort.

She was meant for me.

We passed by the shed and Tally returned the yoga mat, then we continued on to the waterfront restaurant, where the breakfast buffet was being served. There were more people around than there had been the last couple of days, perhaps guests who'd arrived last minute for the wedding later this morning.

There was a small, two-person table in the corner near the restrooms. It wasn't as pretty or romantic as the other spots, but it might be the only choice we had.

I gestured toward it. "I'll save that table. You get food first."

"Sure."

I headed for the table and sat facing into the room. It wasn't long before Tally appeared, her plate stacked with pastries, fresh fruit, and yoghurt. A cup of creamy-colored coffee was clasped in her other hand. She placed her plate and cup down and sank onto the other chair.

I went to put together a breakfast plate for myself. There

were a lot of tempting options, but I was supposed to be behaving, so I served myself eggs on whole wheat toast with a side of granola and Greek yoghurt. Plenty of protein and a few complex carbohydrates. Nowhere near as delicious as Tally's fruit Danishes, but it'd have to do.

I poured a plain black coffee and rejoined Tally. We didn't talk much while we ate, although our gazes caught several times. Once, I winked at her and the sweetest blush swept across her cheeks. Another time, she smiled at me like I'd made her whole day just by existing, and my chest swelled with pride.

By the time we returned to our room, there was nothing I wanted more than to gather her in my arms and spend another day getting to know her in ways I'd never dreamed of.

Unfortunately, we had a wedding ceremony to prepare for.

That said, it wasn't for an hour yet, and it would take me five minutes to put my suit on. Maybe ten if I attempted to style my hair too, although it was so short, there was hardly anything I could do with it.

I settled on the bed and surfed the channels on the TV until I found one showing the NHL's All Stars weekend. I hadn't been invited this year, but I had a feeling it was close. Hopefully next year would be my time. Dad had gone to All Stars on several occasions, and Uncle Wayne had once.

I'd get there too.

While I watched the TV, Tally retreated into the bathroom. The hum of the shower came through the door and a little later, it stopped again.

Time passed quickly and when she emerged forty minutes later, her face was fully made up and her hair was loosely curled and shone in the light filtering through the partially obscured window.

Her lips were even pinker than usual, her eyes bluer, and all of her features just seemed a little *more.*

Not to mention the fact she was naked with every one of her mouthwatering curves on display and that tempting spot between her thighs making me want to reconsider whether we actually needed to attend this wedding.

"You look amazing." In fact, I had no idea how I was supposed to keep my hands off her.

"Thanks." She grinned, pleased, and opened the closet where she'd hung some of her clothing earlier in the week. My gaze traveled down the slope of her back and over her ass, which jiggled enticingly each time she moved.

She pulled out the blue dress and laid it on the bed, then grabbed underwear, the white strappy sandals, the silver pendant necklace, and the white purse to go with the outfit.

I muted the TV, far more interested in the show she was putting on. She slid on a pair of panties and a strapless bra, then stepped into the dress and shimmied it up over her hips.

She turned. "Can you zip this up please?"

I leapt to my feet and rushed over. My fingers trembled as I clumsily took hold of the zipper and drew up the tab to the top, hiding the luminous skin of her back.

She passed me the necklace. "This too."

The delicate clasp was small and I had to close my eyes and count to five to calm myself before sliding the necklace around her neck and fastening it.

Satisfaction pulsed through me. There was just something about dressing Tally in things I'd bought for her that really brought out my caveman impulses. I trailed my hands down her waist and rested them on her hips, taking a moment to kiss the side of her neck.

"Stunning," I murmured.

She twisted toward me and pressed her lips to mine. Hers were slightly sticky and tasted of strawberries. I groaned deep in my chest and rested my hand around the base of her throat. She pulled away and blinked slowly, her eyes a little dazed.

"You're going to smudge my makeup." She didn't sound too bothered by that.

I nuzzled the crook of her shoulder. "You'll still be the sexiest woman here without it."

Laughing, she pushed me away. "It isn't long until the ceremony starts. We need to be ready."

I huffed, knowing she was right. "Fine."

Willing my libido to calm down, I found my suit and put it on, pleased with how the shade of blue complemented Tally's dress. She'd donned her sandals and, based on the shininess of her lips, she must have reapplied whatever she'd had on before I kissed her.

I ducked into the bathroom to check my reflection and, once I was certain I was someone Tally could be proud to be with, I stuffed the key card and my phone into my pocket and held the door open for her.

"Mom asked if we could meet them in their room before we go down," Tally said, tapping away at her phone.

"Are they ready?" I asked.

She nodded.

We headed to their room, where Mrs. Dufresne cooed over how gorgeous Tally looked. Her father didn't say much, beyond remarking the dress suited her, but the paternal gleam in his eyes gave away far more than his words did.

The ceremony was being held on the beach, so we made our way through the resort and around the corner. About half the chairs were occupied and a handful of wedding guests hovered nearby, chatting in groups.

Chris stood with his groomsmen just in front of an arch draped with translucent white curtains. Thick bouquets of white flowers in sturdy vases lined the aisle. Chris was dressed all in white, while the groomsmen wore a shade that was almost pinkish but with brown undertones. The color probably had some fancy name I'd never guess.

We sat in the back row and discussed our travel plans for tomorrow until the seats had filled and a celebrant stood in the front and asked us to rise.

Music played from hidden speakers and Shanna appeared on the edge of the beach, wearing a long dress the same pink-brown color as the groomsmens' outfits. Coral followed behind her, and once they stood in place, Lake glided along the sand, arm in arm with her father, her dress almost blindingly white in the sun with a long veil trailing in her wake.

Lake and her father reached the end of the aisle and she joined Chris and the rest of the wedding party while he sat with his wife. The celebrant instructed us to sit, and the ceremony began.

I didn't pay much attention to what was being said as they recited their vows. Instead, I took Tally's hand in mine and envisioned our future.

I could imagine doing this with her one day. Our ceremony would be quieter. I'd have Keysha prepare the most extravagant chocolate creation that Tally had ever seen. We'd exchange rings, kiss, and dance the night away.

There was a pang in my chest. I wanted that future. Badly.

When the ceremony ended, we waited our turn to congratulate Lake and Chris and then wound through the crowd to the makeshift bar while the photographer began ordering people around. I asked for a glass of champagne for Tally and a sugar-free Coke for myself. We wandered a little farther away, near a cluster of palm trees, and sipped our drinks as we watched the happy couple pose for one photo after another.

"Hey."

I snapped around. Thad stood behind a tree nearby, dressed in board shorts and a T-shirt.

"What are you doing here?" I asked, recalling that Tally had said Coral had kicked him out.

He grinned sharkishly. "Oh, I just wondered whether you enjoyed your treats from the bakery yesterday. Neither of you finished eating, so I thought, perhaps you prefer *fake*, processed junk to high-quality baked goods."

Beside me, Tally sucked in a sharp breath. She'd noticed the emphasis on the word "fake," just as I had.

My brain worked quickly, flipping through yesterday's events and reminding me that we'd been at the bakery when I'd told her I wanted to try a real relationship with her. Had he been there? And had I explicitly said that what we'd had so far was fake?

I couldn't remember seeing him, but I'd been completely preoccupied by her. I couldn't recall my exact wording either.

"What do you want?" Tally demanded, a tremor in her voice. "Why won't you leave me alone? You're the one who cheated on me. I don't get why you won't just go away."

Thad's expression darkened. "Because you ruined what I had with Coral, and I want you to make it right."

"I didn't ruin anything." I stepped toward him, wanting more than ever to plant my fist right between his eyes. "You're the cheating asshole out of the three of us. So fuck off."

Thad rolled his eyes and walked away, but I had a sinking feeling that he wouldn't stay gone for long.

"He knows." Tally buried her face in my chest and whimpered. "Alec, he knows."

"He can't prove anything," I assured her, really fucking hoping that was true. "He just wants to scare you."

"Well, he succeeded." She sniffled. "Do you think anyone heard?"

I looked around but no one seemed to be paying us any attention. "I don't think so. Come on, why don't we get out of here? I'd love to strip you out of that dress."

SEVENTEEN

TALLY

I allowed Alec to lead me away from the beach and through the resort to our private room without making a fuss. I knew I should stay for more of the celebrations, but I just couldn't handle that right now, and despite my tumultuous emotions and my fear of what Thad might do next, I was more than willing to let him distract me.

He swiped his key card, ushered me in, and immediately went to close the curtains. I flicked the light on, grateful the window was ajar, and a gentle breeze stirred the air, because otherwise, it might be overly warm.

"Do you want a massage?" Alec asked. "Or I could get you a drink out of the minibar?"

I frowned. "What happened to stripping me out of my dress?"

He hesitated, toying with the buttons of his shirt. "Thad is an asshole, and he upset you. I wasn't thinking properly when I said that. I'm sure you're not in the mood after dealing with him."

"It's weird, but I kind of am." My cheeks must have been burning, so I ducked my head to hide my embarrassment. He was right. I really shouldn't want sex right now. But his protectiveness turned me on, and I'd let Thad take enough from me already. He wasn't ruining this too. "I mean, fuck him, right? But not actually, because I'd rather fuck you."

That hadn't come out the way I'd meant it. Oh, God. This would be a great time for the floor to swallow me up.

Alec came closer and tilted my chin up. "You want me, cocobug?"

"Yes," I whispered, loving his spicy citrus scent.

He smirked. "You want me to fill you up and fuck you until you can't think of anything other than me?"

"That would be nice, yes."

He laughed. "It'll be more than nice." He paused for a moment, his expression turning serious. "If you want to stop at any time, just tell me. Even if it's just for a few minutes."

I nodded, too scared to speak in case my voice broke.

He knelt in front of me, one knee on the ground and the other foot planted. "Put your foot on my thigh."

I did as he said and he brushed my skirt out of the way and slowly removed my sandal, peppering kisses up my calf. I shivered. I'd never have guessed that my leg could be such an erogenous zone.

When he discarded the sandal, I switched feet, and he took his time sliding off the other one, his fingertips caressing the sensitive skin as he trailed kisses from my ankle to my knee. The sandal fell by the wayside and he edged up my skirt, nuzzling the soft skin of my inner thigh, the slight rasp of his stubble setting my nerves alight in the best way.

He eased down my panties and kissed the top of my mound, then ventured lower, his lips and tongue teasing my clit and delving deeper. I ran my hands over his hair, blissfully distracted, unable to think of anything other than him and the riot of sensations he stirred in me.

"Bed," he growled against my sensitive flesh.

I melted backward with no idea how my legs didn't fall out from under me. My ass hit the mattress and Alec hitched the skirt up to my hips and descended on me with the single-minded determination to drive me completely out of my wits.

He tormented me and teased me, bringing me to the edge of orgasm only to ease off over and over again. It felt so good, but I wanted more, and I couldn't decide whether to throttle him for not giving me enough to send me flying or beg and plead for him to do just that.

I settled for somewhere in between. "If you don't fuck me in the next thirty seconds, I'm going to scream bloody murder."

He raised his head, his eyes pitch black and his lips glistening. "Scream all you like."

"Oh, my God, you're impossible."

Chuckling huskily, he stood and undressed, revealing that gorgeous, inked body I'd already come to adore.

I sat up enough to pull the skirt out from underneath myself and struggled my way out of the dress and bra, not nearly as seductive as him with his low-key strip tease. I clambered up and pulled him onto the bed, pivoting us as he fell so that he landed on his back with me hovering over him.

As soon as he was flat on the bed, I straddled him, rubbing my wet pussy against his hard, straining cock.

"Fuck." His hands fisted at his sides. "You feel so. Damn. Good."

I rode his length, moving my hips in a sultry way that might have made me self-conscious if not for the lust blazing in his eyes as he stared up at me. His jaw tensed and my lips twisted with satisfaction.

He wasn't the only one who could tempt and tease.

But soon, the need pulsing through me became too much. It wasn't as fun to tease myself as it was to do it to him. I scrambled off him, searched for a condom and found one. I tore the foil, rolled it down his cock, and positioned myself above him.

"Take me inside you," he demanded.

I dropped onto him in one smooth motion. A groan tore from his throat and he grabbed my hips.

"Please, Tally." His Adam's apple bobbled as his fingers tightened instinctively. "Use me. Take what you need."

Encouraged by his desperation and dirty words, I began to ride him, slowly at first, dragging out every ounce of enjoyment, but as the thread of desire drew tighter within me, my movements became faster and more urgent.

He spurred me on with grunts and moans, curses and kisses. Pressure built and I cried out, throwing my head back.

"That's it, baby. You have such sexy tits."

He cupped them between his palms, kneading them and tonguing my nipples. Heat rocketed through me, and I grabbed his shoulders and pressed my lips to his in a passionate kiss as a tidal wave of pleasure slammed into me and I shuddered around him.

His cock pulsed inside me and our tongues tangled as I felt him thicken and jerk, coming with a low growl.

I sprawled on his chest, panting heavily. His cock slipped out of me. We'd need to deal with the mess in a moment, but for now, I was content to lie with my heart hammering against his, basking in an intimate moment the likes of which I'd never imagined I'd get to share with him.

Eventually, our sweat began to cool and the need to clean up outweighed the pleasantness of our embrace. I slid off him and gave myself a quick wash while he dealt with the condom and his own situation.

He joined me in the shower and my "quick wash" turned

into a steamy make out session followed by another round of lovemaking.

We spent the day wrapped up in each other, heedless of the outside world. Eventually, we drifted to sleep.

If we'd known what the morning would bring, we might have slept a lot less peacefully.

EIGHTEEN

TALLY

Pounding on the bedroom door jarred me from a pleasant dream about all the things Alec liked to do with his tongue.

I sat up and brushed my hair off my face. "What's going on?"

Beside me, Alec already had his legs off the side of the bed. He bent, snatched up a shirt and tossed it to me. "Put that on."

I slipped the shirt over my head, self-conscious because I was well-endowed, so the fact I wasn't wearing a bra was exceedingly obvious. I crossed my arms and hoped that whoever was bashing the door down had come to the wrong room.

I glanced at the clock. It was only 7:30 a.m. Check out wasn't for another couple of hours. There was no reason for anyone to be hassling us.

Alec pulled on a pair of shorts and went to the door. "What?" he growled as he opened it.

Three people spilled into the room. First was Coral, her face a mess of tears and snot, a tablet clutched in her hands.

Second was Mom, her expression uncharacteristically somber. In the rear, Dad entered wearing the same glower I imagined he used to make the opposition tremble in court.

Coral pushed past Alec, stumbling over one of our suitcases, and dropped onto the edge of the bed. She thrust the tablet at me. "You need to see this."

Startled, and more than a little confused, I took the tablet from her and studied the screen. Immediately, I jolted awake. Taking up the upper two thirds of the screen was a photograph of me wrapped in Alec's arms on the beach. We were wearing our outfits from the wedding ceremony yesterday and, if I looked carefully at the blurred out backgrounds, I thought I could make out the silhouettes of other wedding guests.

My gaze dropped to the headline beneath the photograph.

Alec Wright's Sham Relationship.

I blinked, praying to whatever god might be listening that I'd read it wrong, but the words didn't change.

"Oh, God," I whimpered.

Alec reached for the tablet and took it from me.

Everyone knew the truth. Or, if they didn't, they soon would.

What had we done?

Alec swore.

I needed to know exactly what the article said. I plucked the tablet from Alec's grasp and scrolled down the page. My horror grew as I read more. Somehow, they knew everything— or at least, enough to humiliate us completely.

Although...contrary to how it looked at first glance, the writer hadn't been totally negative where Alec was concerned. She emphasized how swoony it was for the famous NHL wing to step up and help his best friend in her time of need, even if his actions were misguided.

Somehow, the article managed to present him as a white

knight while making me out to be completely pathetic. A woman who couldn't keep her boyfriend happy.

She identified me as the owner of Coco Luxe and went on to scathingly question what kind of self-respecting business-woman would stoop low enough to bat her eyelashes at a man and ask him to solve her problems.

She called my professional reputation into question.

It was awful.

"How did this happen?" I asked numbly.

"I'm sorry!" Coral buried her face in her hands, her shoulders shaking. "I didn't realize he'd actually do it."

Alec scowled. "Who?"

His tone made it clear that he knew exactly who was responsible for this.

"Thad." She dropped her hands and grabbed mine, knocking the tablet onto the bed. "He told me that he overheard you guys talking at the bakery. He seemed so angry, and I don't understand why, but honestly, I wasn't really listening because I was just so sick of his bullshit."

I pulled my hands away and closed my eyes. "He probably hoped that telling you what he'd overheard would make us look bad, so you'd take him back, thinking him a victim in some way. It's twisted, but it's the sort of logic he'd believe in."

She snorted wetly. "Yeah, instead it only made me feel even worse. I mean, the fact that you'd feel the need to do whatever it was that you did because you were so scared about seeing us. That's really crappy."

"So, did he do this out of spite?" Mom asked, obviously trying her best to follow the conversation even though she'd gotten lost a few turns back.

Coral grimaced. "Maybe partly, but he lost his job too, so he probably thought he could cash in on it, since Alec is kinda famous and all."

My mouth fell open. "He lost his job? When?"

Her forehead creased. "Maybe six weeks ago."

Before we'd broken up. Perhaps that was why he'd seemed so unsatisfied and desperate for me to spend more time with him. Maybe, in a way, it was even why he'd cheated. It would have been a balm for his ego to be able to have two women at once.

"I don't give a fucking shit if his whole family died," Alec growled, stalking the length of the room. "It doesn't give him the right to do this. Especially since he didn't even get the facts right."

I watched his feet as he stomped across the floor. I got the feeling that any omission from Thad had likely been out of pettiness rather than simply being wrong. If he'd overheard our conversation at the bakery then he had to have known that we're together for real now. He left that part out when he'd spoken to the reporter because it would have made me look less pathetic.

He was aiming for maximum humiliation, and potentially threatening the reputation of the business I'd worked so hard to build—the one he'd resented for getting between us.

Oh, God, would this mean fewer customers for Coco Luxe?

Did my customers actually read this trash? And if so, how should I even start doing damage control?

I didn't have a plan for this. I'd never thought I'd need to. I wasn't famous. Just a woman who loved making chocolates.

"I never want to see that man again," I said.

"You won't," Coral rushed to assure me. "At least, not because of me. I've already blocked him on everything. I hope you have too."

"Actually, no." My voice was small. "He never tried to contact me, so it didn't occur to me."

Alec cleared his throat. "Uh, about that. I might have

blocked his number on your phone while you were asleep the night after the breakup. Coral's too."

"Oh." And here I'd just thought he hadn't cared enough to reach out. Honestly, I was grateful I hadn't had to deal with that, so I supposed Alec had done me a favor. Actually, he'd done me several, and all I'd brought into his life was drama. If this could damage my business, I hated to think what it might mean for him. "I'm so sorry for dragging you into my mess."

He cocked his head. "You're not mad?"

I shrugged. I was too busy feeling defeated. I didn't have the emotional bandwidth to be angry too.

"Also, you have nothing to apologize for." He ushered Coral out of the way and sat beside me. "This was my idea. It's my fault it's happened. I'm the one who's sorry."

A sigh escaped me. "You were trying to help."

Dad circled around in front of us and knelt so he could look me in the eyes. "Whatever is going on, we're here for you. Do you want me to sue the guy for slander? I could keep him tied up in courtrooms for the next year."

A smile tugged at the corner of my mouth. "No, but thank you for offering."

"If you change your mind, I'll be here. In the meantime, what do you need from us?"

"I don't know..." Everything had happened so quickly. Only a few minutes ago, I'd been sleeping peacefully, and now my life had been turned upside down.

Did all the wedding guests know? What about the hotel staff? Were they gossiping even now?

"Do you think you could find out whether everyone is talking about it?" I asked quietly.

His face softened. "Sure thing."

He and Mom turned to leave.

Alec wrapped his arms around me. "You'll be okay. We'll

get through this. We know we're really together, and soon enough, everyone else will realize it too."

Mom scoffed. "Of course you are. No one who sees you together could ever think it's fake."

Dad tugged her arm and they stepped outside and closed the door softly behind them.

I dragged in a deep breath and let it out in one go. "Thank you, Coral. I appreciate you letting us all know about this, so I wasn't ambushed."

Coral frowned. "It's literally the least I could do after all the pain I caused you."

I nodded. I didn't have the energy to discuss the matter further, and I wasn't really sure I wanted to either. "Could Alec and I have a little time alone?"

"Sure." She scuttled to the door and hesitated before waving awkwardly and letting herself out.

I felt Alec's gaze on the side of my face and turned.

"You're really not angry with me?" he asked. "This is my fault. It was my idea to pretend to be together. You said no, but I talked you into it. Then there's the fact that no one would have even cared about the truth if I wasn't semi-famous just because I chase a puck down the ice for a living."

"Don't be ridiculous." My nerves were scraped too raw for me to mince words. "I agreed to the plan, and you can't help the fact that some people find you interesting. You didn't ask for that. I'm not angry at you. I'm just...upset, and scared about what might happen now. This article makes me look really bad. Will my business suffer?"

He nuzzled the side of my head. "We'll make sure it doesn't. Somehow. I promise. I'll stand by your side for every second and we'll get through this. Coco Luxe will too. I'm so sorry, Tally. I never meant for this to happen."

"You've said that already." I sighed. "I'll survive." I wasn't about to say that it was okay, because it wasn't. It sucked. This whole fake relationship had started out because I wanted to keep my dignity intact, and now it was not only cracked but completely shattered, along with my reputation.

On the nightstand, Alec's phone rang. He ignored it, holding me close and murmuring nonsense in my ear.

It rang again.

"You'd better get that."

He looked over. "It's my agent. He can wait."

"Maybe he'll have some ideas about how to make the most of this." Not that it necessarily painted Alec in a bad light, but I couldn't imagine his agent was pleased that he'd gotten himself embroiled in a scandal like this.

"Are you sure?" he asked.

"Yeah. Answer it."

He released me for long enough to grab the phone and then held onto it with one hand while he kept me close with the other. I shut my eyes and tried not to think about what might be going on outside or what the world thought of me.

I was tempted to open my social media—or perhaps Coco Luxe's—to see if it had been flooded by unpleasant comments and messages but decided I couldn't handle that. Instead, I grabbed my phone and sent Keysha a message to warn her about what had happened, so she'd be prepared for whatever she might face at the shop, then I laid back and listened to Alec and his agent talk damage control strategies.

Guilt churned in my gut. I knew it was hypocritical of me to feel guilty considering he felt guilty too and I'd assured him he had no reason to. The fact remained that if not for me, neither of us would be in this mess. If I hadn't dated such a terrible guy, none of this would have happened.

Although that would mean that Alec and I wouldn't have

gotten together either, and I could never wish that undone, so I supposed we just had to deal with the consequences.

There was a knock at the door. I pulled away from Alec and went to open it. Mom and Dad stood on the other side. Mom glanced past me, noticing that Alec was on the phone.

"We didn't hear anyone discussing it yet," she said quietly. "If you leave here soon, you might be able to get home before too many people read the article."

A little of the tightness in my chest eased.

"Thanks." I held the door wide, so they could enter. "I'm going to pack."

Behind me, Alec ended his call.

"I'm going to find that good-for-nothing asshole," he growled, stomping past Dad and out the door. I doubted he'd find Thad. My ex was probably on his way back to the mainland by now, or perhaps he'd even flown out last night.

Mom helped me pack while Dad hovered awkwardly near the door. When Alec came back, he'd deflated a little and muttered something about not having been able to track Thad down. It was probably for the best. I didn't want him to do anything that might get him into trouble.

"I don't care about Thad." I rested my head on his chest and closed my eyes, emotionally exhausted even though the day had only just begun. "Can we just go home?"

NINETEEN

ALEC

I opened the front door of my house and smiled at the couple on the doorstep. "Mr. and Mrs. Dufresne, thanks for coming."

Mrs. Dufresne rolled her eyes. "I've told you to call me Daisy."

"Thank you for inviting us," Mr. Dufresne said, offering me a bottle of wine.

I took the bottle and thanked him. He smoothed his palms down the front of his neat, white-striped suit—he must have come straight from work—and asked, "Is Tally here yet?"

"Not yet. According to Keysha, they should be about five minutes away."

"Perfect."

I moved aside and they stepped into the foyer. The hum of chatter filtered through from the living room. "Everyone else is through there."

They followed my gesture and preceded me to the living area, where most of my team, their partners, and my family were already gathered. I'd had to buy extra seating because the sofa and pair of armchairs I'd had came nowhere near to fitting everyone.

Mr. and Mrs. Dufresne joined my parents near the kitchen and Mom offered them each a drink. I'd forewarned all the parents about my plan for the evening, which had required me to come clean about how Tally and I really had been pretending at the beginning. It had been uncomfortable but I didn't want them to be blindsided.

They'd taken it well, although I could tell Mom, in particular, was bothered by our deception. I hated that, but all I could do now was be honest and hope that would be enough to earn her forgiveness.

I placed the bottle of wine from Mr. Dufresne on the counter and wandered over to the door closest to the front of the house, so I'd be able to hear when the next car arrived.

"Nervous?" my sister, Jane, asked from her cross-legged position on an armchair.

"A little." I spoke quietly. I didn't mind Jane knowing that I was anxious—out of anyone, she would understand—but I'd rather not get ribbed about it by my teammates.

"You'll be fine." Her brown eyes were warm and encouraging. "You and Tally are perfect for each other. It's going to work out."

I hoped so.

I couldn't deny that the fact Tally had been holed up in her apartment since we'd returned on Sunday worried me. According to Keysha, they'd had some hate on social media—which I was certain Tally was agonizing over—but nothing particularly troublesome happening at the shop itself, with the exception of a couple of cancelled orders that were small enough they didn't really harm the bottom line.

Still, Tally seemed afraid to trust that things would work out.

I'd visited her after training each day but I still wasn't completely sure what was going on in her mind other than a big, messy shame spiral. I just hoped that, whatever it was, she'd find my surprise sweet rather than embarrassing.

My stomach knotted. "What if I got it wrong?"

"Then you'll fix it," Jane said simply.

I wished I had as much faith in myself as she did.

The doorbell rang. The knots in my gut tightened. That must be them.

"All right, everyone." I raised my voice to be heard. "We're on."

The chatter died momentarily before starting back up, this time with a more excited edge to it. A little uncertain about whether I'd done the right thing, I went to the door and opened it, a chasm of doubt looming ahead of me.

Tally greeted me with a smile, but her eyes were fogged with confusion. "What's going on? Keysha insisted on driving me here after work and I have no idea what's happening."

Beside her, Keysha smirked. "I did my part. Time for you to do yours."

"Thanks, Key." I flashed her a grin. I really was appreciative to her for getting Tally here. "Feel free to stay. There's plenty of food."

"Food?" Tally's confusion deepened.

I ushered Keysha past her, into the house, but remained in the doorway with Tally. "I'm having a bit of a gathering. There's, uh, going to be a surprise for you later."

Please don't let her be mad.

A furrow formed between her brows. "A surprise? Like what?"

I took her hand. "You'll have to wait and see. Come in. We've been cooking all afternoon."

The place smelled incredible. Even better than it usually did during our postgame dinners. Mom, Dad, and I had gone all out, and in addition to the home cooked food, there was also a selection of baked treats from a nearby bakery and a platter of Tally's favorite chocolates, provided by Keysha.

Tally followed me into the living room. Mom had finished arranging platters of food along the kitchen counter and plates, glasses, cutlery, and drinks were on the dining table. I chose a plate and began to fill it at the counter. When I handed it to her, she watched me, obviously baffled.

"For you," I said.

She took the plate and headed to the sofa, which had thoughtfully been left clear. Jane leaned over and said something to her. I let everyone know they could grab whatever they liked, then I filled my own plate and sat beside Tally.

Tally bumped my shoulder. "I've had three people tell me how glad they are that we're together."

Jane nodded. "I was just telling Tally that as soon as I heard, I knew that the journalist was wrong about it being fake, no matter how it might have started out. You two belong together."

My heart warmed and I held Jane's gaze, silently thanking her for putting Tally at ease. My sister may not be outgoing, but there was something about her that calmed those around her.

"Of course it's real," Gallagher said, flopping cross-legged onto the floor in front of us. "I knew you two were destined for each other when Alec warned us to back off."

Tally's eyebrows flew up. "He what?"

"Oh, yeah. He said we were all a bunch of fuckboys and that if any of us touched you, he'd..." He trailed off, apparently catching sight of my glare. "But hey! All's well that ends well, right?"

Tally stared at me. My face heated and my shoulders crept up to my ears as embarrassment set in. In hindsight, it was obvious that I'd wanted Tally long before I admitted it, even to myself.

"You're mine," I murmured, flushing deeper.

She shook her head, chuckling. "Apparently so. Alec, what *is* all of this?"

I scratched my jaw, the bristles rasping against my fingertips. "I might have, kind of, done something. Just watch."

Across the room, Dexter switched on the TV, which I'd already connected to the appropriate talk show.

Everyone fell silent.

On the screen, the hostess—a middle-aged blonde with a pixie cut—invited me to sit on the sofa opposite her. I was wearing the same ocean blue suit I'd worn to Lake's wedding, which I hoped would make me come across as fun rather than a show pony.

"Oh, my God." Tally turned to me, her lips parted, eyes wide. "Seriously, what's going on? You were on—" She cut herself off, her hands covering her mouth.

"Listen," I urged, shifting closer to her so that our bodies were pressed together from knee to hip to shoulder.

The hostess introduced me to the audience and settled more comfortably onto her seat. She crossed one leg over the other and rested her palms on them.

"So, Alec," she began, leaning slightly toward me, "rumor has it you're not really off the market, is that right?"

"That is absolutely not correct," I said crisply.

Someone in the living room cheered.

"I'm in a very committed relationship with a woman who

has been my best friend for many years. There's nothing I wouldn't do for her."

The hostess's eyes twinkled. "Including a nationwide interview, when you're a notoriously private person?"

I nodded. "Including that."

She whistled. "She must be special."

"She is."

In real time, Tally shuffled closer. "I can't believe you did this! When did you even have the time?"

"Coach let me out of practice this morning," I whispered back. "He'll probably kick my ass for it in training tomorrow, but he knew this was important to me."

On the screen, the hostess asked me about Tally, and I explained who she was, how we'd met as teenagers, and the truth of how I'd fallen for my best friend bit by bit over the years but was too foolish to see it until I'd seen what I could have with her.

I took a brief detour to talk about her delicious chocolate creations and how they were my absolute favorite to indulge in during the off-season, hoping that would ease some of Tally's concerns about her business.

Finally, I relived the kiss that changed everything. Several of the women present swooned.

"So, what does this mean for your hockey?" the hostess asked.

The virtual version of me straightened. "Just that it's no longer my number one priority. I love hockey and always will. I'll give it everything I can. After all, I want a championship ring. But Tally comes first. Always."

"Do you mean that?" Tally asked, her eyes shining.

"Every word." I watched her face, wondering what she made of all of this. Had airing my love for her to the entire nation been too much? Was she embarrassed? Or did she like that I'd been willing to do that for her?

Whatever the case was, I couldn't bring myself to regret it. I'd put everything on the line for love and I was proud of that.

"I—" She started to speak, but when the hostess asked me about the man who'd gone running to the tabloids about our fake relationship, she spun back to the TV.

I smirked as I watched the recorded version of me tell the whole country what a vindictive, cheating asshole Thad was, spewing toxic bullshit to anyone who would listen because he was furious that she'd had the audacity to move on and find someone better than him.

Tally clapped her hand to her mouth a few seconds too late to hide her laughter.

"Wait for it," I murmured.

A moment later, a photograph of Thad appeared behind the hostess. It was terrible. His face was twisted like he'd sniffed shit, and his cheeks were red from sunburn.

A snort burst from Tally. "Oh, no!"

A spiteful wave of glee rose within me. "Oh, yes."

The photo had come from Coral, who'd been pissed at how he'd behaved during her sister's wedding and eager to make amends for what she'd done, in any way possible.

Finally, the interview ended. The room was startlingly silent, with over a dozen pairs of eyes on us.

I waited for Tally's reaction, my heart in my throat.

Her lips curved in a wide smile. "I can't believe you did all this."

"What do you think?" I asked, nerves rioting through me.

"I think you're crazy, but that was the sweetest thing anyone has done for me." Her eyes sparkled and I had the almost irresistible urge to kiss her.

"You're worth it," I told her. "I'm falling in love with you Tally, and I want the whole world to know."

But mostly, I wanted *her* to know, and to never have any reason to doubt me. Hopefully, this would help with that.

Her expression was fond as she wound her arms around my neck. "Oh, you sweet, ridiculous man. I'm falling for you too."

With that, she kissed me while our guests whooped and cheered.

I smiled against her mouth, my heart beating furiously. "Be mine, Tally?"

"Forever."

TWENTY

TALLY

I shouted and jumped up and down as Alec skated out onto the ice in the T-Mobile Arena in Las Vegas. It was a little more than a month after his televised interview and it was the first time this season that his parents and I had managed to make it to one of his away games.

The atmosphere in the arena was electric. Thousands of hockey fans screamed support for their team and many of them held banners or signs. The three of us could have been lost in the masses if not for our position right above and behind the penalty box.

Alec glided around the inside of the rink, scanning the crowd. I could tell when he spotted us because he dipped his head in acknowledgement and shifted his focus to the warm-up.

"Are you excited?" his mom asked near my ear.

"Of course! I can't wait to see him get out there and kill it."

Her lips twisted ruefully. "Has it occurred to you that this is the first away game you've gone to as a couple?"

"Yeah." Not that I saw why it mattered. Whether I was his best friend or his girlfriend, I was there to shout myself hoarse cheering for my favorite guy.

Mr. Wright offered me his fries, but I shook my head. I wasn't hungry yet, although I was sure I would be soon. Fortunately, there were plenty of snack options.

On the ice, Alec performed drills with his fellow first line forwards. Each time he slipped the puck past Davi, I clapped, even though I doubted he could hear me. It made me feel like I was supporting him in spirit, even if he wasn't conscious of my physical presence at every second.

They added a defender into the drill, and then another. After a while, the teams prepared to start and all but the starting lineup cleared off the ice. As expected, Alec was in the front line on the right.

The puck dropped and Vegas beat Cromwell to it, zigzagging up the ice. Alec tried to steal the puck from the Vegas center, but he passed it off to the wing, who shot it back to the defense, who sent it straight back to the center, who was not clear to take a shot at goal. Fortunately, Davi knocked the puck aside.

The game was tight. By the end of the first period, there was no score. The second period was more hands on, with a few players being roughly checked into the boards and a fist-fight breaking out. It ended with no points on the board.

Entering the third period, both teams went in fast and hard. I could tell from watching Alec that he was tired, but he didn't flag, and the coach didn't swap out the first line despite how much game time they'd had. He wanted to win as badly as the players did.

One of Vegas's wings broke away and rocketed down the side of the rink with the puck. Dexter cross-checked him and the puck zinged away, ricocheting off the side.

Cromwell took control of the puck and charged up the center. Alec raced alongside him, gathering speed. Cromwell was heading for a confrontation with the defense. He caught Alec's eye a millisecond before he flicked him the puck, and quicker than the goalie could react, my boyfriend slotted it past him, across the line and into the net.

The Dragons' fans roared and clapped. Alec scanned the crowd and seemed to lock his attention onto us briefly before he continued to play.

After that, with a goal on the board and none for the opposition, the Dragons hung farther back, shoring up the defense to make sure Vegas didn't have a chance of scoring. Alec's parents and I counted down the minutes until the whistle blew, the timer stopped counting down, and it was official. We'd won.

On the ice, Cromwell slammed into Alec, slinging his arm around his shoulder. Alec hugged him back and then pushed him away lightly, circling around to congratulate each of his teammates in turn. The guys who'd been on the bench loaded onto the ice and the next thirty seconds were a whirl of whoops as they celebrated.

Once the excitement died down, Alec circled around to the penalty box, tore off his helmet, and blew a kiss at me. My heart fluttered. My cheeks must have been fire engine red as I caught the kiss and blew him one back, using both of my hands to send it winging toward him.

He was so sweet. God, I adored him.

The players cooled down. We vacated the stands, hoping to exchange a few words with Alec on his way to the changeroom, but his coach had caught him, and their heads were together as they talked.

We waited outside, but when Alec re-emerged, he didn't join us. Instead, he walked alongside Coach Alan, clad in a smart navy suit and a white shirt that brought out the glowing tan of his skin. He slipped me a secret smile as they passed.

"He must be doing press," his Mom said, a complicated mix of disappointment and excitement crossing her face. No doubt she was disappointed she'd have to wait to hug her son but thrilled he'd been chosen as the team's ambassador for the day.

We followed the pair to the media room and watched from outside as they fielded questions. Alec spoke well, but that shouldn't be surprising considering he'd had a lifetime of experience.

One of the reporters near the back spotted us through the glass and seemed to be deciding whether to sneak out and try to get a sound bite from either me or Alec's dad, a former NHL great. Fortunately, Coach Alan spoke at that moment, capturing her attention.

"We'll take one last question," he said.

"Yeah." Alec grinned. "Much as I like talking to you guys, the love of my life is waiting."

My heart lifted, and my soul felt light. He meant me. That gorgeous, successful man loved *me*.

Several hands flew up. Coach Alan pointed at a short, slim woman near the front.

She cleared her throat. "Your next game is against the Chicago Chaos. What do you expect the outcome to be?"

Alec stayed silent, letting Coach Alan respond.

"The Chaos aren't having a particularly clean season," the coach said, surprisingly tactfully. Everyone knew the Chaos were a hot mess. "We're playing well, and I see no reason why we shouldn't win the game. Thank you all for coming, and for your support."

He backed away from the microphone and gestured toward the door. Alec went ahead of him. As soon as he strode into the corridor, I raced over to him and threw myself into his arms. He closed them around me and kissed me. Something flashed around us—perhaps the photographers trying to capture a feel-good moment. We both ignored them.

"I love you," he said against my lips, echoing his earlier sentiment from during the interview.

I snuggled closer, soaking in the comfort provided by his broad chest. "I love you too."

He gazed into my eyes, and everything inside me settled. All felt right with the world. I was in love with my best friend and he loved me back. Not many people were as lucky as us.

"Let's get out of here," he murmured.

I took his hand, more than happy to follow him anywhere. "I thought you'd never ask."

EPILOGUE – JUNE, THE FOLLOWING YEAR

ALEC

The sun beamed down on us from a clear blue sky as I pulled into a park in front of Tranquility Bay Resort.

Tally angled herself toward me, a furrow between her brows betraying her confusion. "Here?"

I turned the key to kill the engine. She'd allowed me to surprise her with this postseason getaway to Hawaii. She'd insisted on knowing our destination but had let me keep the details to myself, such as the hotel we'd be staying at.

I took her hand. "I know this place might have some bad memories for you, so if you want to leave, that's okay, but it's also where we got together. We shared so many of our firsts as a couple here, and I wouldn't trade those for anything."

Her expression softened. "This is perfect. I hardly even remember the not-so-great parts of our last stay here anymore. We never did get back to that bakery either, and I'd love to visit it again."

We got out and unloaded our suitcases. It was summer now and much hotter than it had been during our previous stay, so a line of sweat sprang up on my forehead almost immediately. To be fair, it might not only be the heat making me sweat. The nerves weren't helping matters.

We entered the lobby, gave our bags to a bellhop, and approached the same receptionist we'd met last time we were here.

He grinned. "Alec Wright and his beautiful lady. We're so pleased to have you back."

"It's nice to be here again," Tally replied.

He checked us in, handed us key cards, and gestured to a woman behind him, who stepped forward with a tray of fruity cocktails and passed us one each. Tally glanced at me, one of her eyebrows floating up.

I sipped my drink, acting like it wasn't a big deal. The cocktail wasn't my usual preference but it was nice enough. Tally smiled as she tried hers, her shoulders relaxing a little more. She seemed to get more into the spirit of our summer vacation with each mile that separated us from everyday life.

I gestured toward the rear door that led through to the resort. "Let's walk by the water. They'll take our bags to our room so there's no rush for us to be there."

"That sounds nice."

We wandered through the resort together, taking the paths between the pools and areas of greenery until we reached the waterfront restaurant where we'd shared our first kiss last year.

Acoustic guitar music played from a hidden speaker and a lone table sat in the center of the open-walled area with the thatched roof. Two glasses of champagne sat in front of chairs on opposite sides of the table, and a platter of handcrafted specialty chocolates occupied the center.

Tally faltered. "What's this?"

I dropped to one knee and her eyes widened even further. I reached into my pocket and withdrew the small square box I'd spent the entire duration of our flight fondling.

I popped the lid open to reveal a white gold engagement ring with three princess cut diamonds set into a flat band on the top of the ring. I'd chosen this ring knowing that anything too unwieldy would impede her job, since she worked with her hands a lot. Hopefully, she'd be able to wear this one during the workday.

My heart beat against my ribcage and my mouth was dry. Even though it must be obvious what I was doing considering the whole ring and on-bended-knee thing, it was a struggle to find the right words.

"I love you, Tallulah Dufresne." I held her gaze, my stomach knotted even as my chest overflowed with warmth and affection. "You mean everything to me. You're my best friend, my favorite person to spend time with, and the most wonderful woman I've ever had the honor to know. Will you marry me?"

Love shone in her eyes as she stared at me, her fingertips pressed to her lips.

"Yes," she breathed. "I would love to."

"Give me your hand."

She offered me her left hand and I slipped the ring into place. A perfect fit.

Just like us.

I stood and swept her into a kiss, bending her over my arm and loving the way her curves molded against the planes of my body. Soft meeting hard. Gruff meeting sweet. So different, and yet so right for each other.

I straightened, easing her back to her feet. "I can't wait for you to be my wife."

A smile lit her face. "Let's have a Hawaiian wedding!"

"By the beach, with only our closest friends and family?" I asked.

"It's like you read my mind."

I laughed. "That's what years of friendship will do."

She interlinked her fingers with mine and we walked toward the table together, the sun streaming down, heating my shoulders. I held out her chair and kissed her cheek before releasing her and sitting opposite.

I was so lucky to have her, and I intended to make sure she knew it every day for the rest of our lives.

"Love you, cocobug."

THE END

EXCERPT FROM HEARTLESS AS PUCK

AUSTIN

I'd barely stepped onto the stairs overlooking the ice when Drew McKinley slammed into me as if I were on an opposing team and made a run at the goal.

I turned, instinctively pulling my assistant, Jane, close to absorb the impact with my own body. I fought the need to wrap my arms around her and breathe in her delicate floral scent.

She works for you, jackass. Don't make her uncomfortable.

"Watch it," Drew barked, stomping off like he hadn't just tried to knock me down the stairs.

I ignored him. He might be looking for a fight like always, but I had bigger things on my mind.

"You all right?" I asked Jane as I reluctantly drew back and scanned her face for any indication of distress.

"Fine." She tucked a lock of chocolate-colored hair behind her ear and offered me a shy smile. "Drew doesn't bother me."

I hesitated but decided to take her at her word. After all, very little seemed to ruffle her composure. It made me wonder where she'd learned to remain so level-headed.

I started walking and Jane kept pace. Long-simmering frustration heated my gut. Drew was an asshole, but he was only a symptom of a greater problem. The team's leadership was toxic. I liked to think that I could improve the situation if I was made captain, but unless the coaching staff and management changed, that was probably nothing more than baseless optimism.

Ahead of us, the men's bathroom door opened and Nick Kelly stepped out. He glanced our way and eyes the same shade of blue as the ice in the rink crinkled at the corners.

We drew level with him, and he clapped me on the shoulder. "Good to see you, man. It's been too long." He fell into step with us. "What do you think this big meeting is about?"

I shrugged. "No idea, but I'm curious."

"Perhaps it's supposed to be a pep talk?" Nick suggested, grabbing the meeting room door and holding it open.

I snorted. "Has Coach ever given a pep talk in his life?"

Nick glanced around, checking who was present before he replied. "Only if shouting 'get your head in the fucking game' counts as a pep talk."

My gaze skimmed over the others in the room, and tension eased from my neck when I realized that neither the captain nor alternate captain was here yet. A few of the younger players were hovering over a snack table against one wall.

I gestured toward a sofa on the opposite side of the room. "Over there?"

Nick grimaced. "Probably for the best."

We were both getting older and followed strict diets. We shouldn't tempt ourselves by sitting too near the snacks. As we crossed the room, one of my teammates from last year raised his hand in greeting and I nodded in return.

I flopped onto the sofa and Nick lowered himself down

beside me, then bumped my knee with his and jerked his head toward the far wall. "Have you met that guy yet?"

"What guy?"

He gestured toward the food table, where a rookie player was towering over Jane—who apparently hadn't followed us—getting closer to her than was appropriate. She'd ducked her head and her body language made it perfectly clear that she didn't want to be anywhere near him.

Anger sizzled through me.

"No," I muttered, pushing myself upright. "I don't think Jane knows him either."

Even if she did, she obviously didn't like him. I stalked over to them, my glare burning a hole in the rookie's back. Not that he seemed to notice.

I edged around him and put myself between him and Jane. Up close, I could see what a baby face he had. I doubted he was even over twenty. He must have balls of steel to hit on Jane with me right here.

I met his gaze. "Back off."

He arched an eyebrow. "Is she your girlfriend? I thought this meeting was for players only."

"She's my assistant. She's here for work and deserves to be respected. Consider her off-limits." I kept my voice low and steady. It wasn't his fault he hadn't known that, even if his behavior was unacceptable.

Most assistants didn't attend team meetings, but Jane was invaluable to managing my schedule and keeping a track of my life, so I always insisted she be present unless specifically forbidden by the higher-ups. I wanted to be the best player I could, and she was an important part of that.

The rookie held up his hands defensively. "My bad." He turned back to Jane. "Sorry. Maybe I can make it up—"

"No," I snapped and shuffled Jane past him and back to the

sofa, determined that she wouldn't have to tolerate another second of unwanted attention.

She sat and rifled through her bag, pulling out a tablet and turning it on. I hesitated, an apology on my lips, but she studiously ignored me, and I got the feeling she was annoyed with me for some reason.

I opened my mouth to speak, but before I could say a word, a whistle pierced the room and silence fell.

Assistant Coach Willets stood in front of the glass wall that overlooked the ice, his shoulders tense, his rangy frame stretched to its full height.

"Welcome." He tried to smile, but it didn't reach his eyes. "Thank you all for coming in this morning. We have several important announcements to make, and I'd appreciate it if you could save your questions until the end. Understood?"

A murmur of ascent rippled around the room. My stomach tightened. Exactly what was going on?

"As you might have heard, there will be several significant changes this season." He put his hands behind his back, perhaps to hide the way he was fidgeting. "First off, I want to make it very clear that everything said within this meeting is confidential. You may tell your agents but no one else. If I learn that someone has spoken out of turn, there will be consequences."

I exchanged a look with Nick. I could only imagine what kind of consequences he'd dream up. I liked the guy, but he knew how to work a player until they almost broke.

Willets scanned the room, pausing briefly on each of us. "A few weeks ago, the Chicago Chaos was bought by Joseph Trent."

My breath caught. What?

"Under Trent's ownership," Willets continued, without

giving anyone a chance to react, "we'll be instituting some changes to the coaching staff and the players."

My head spun. Holy shit. Did the fact that Willets was giving this talk mean that one of those changes had been removing the problematic head coach?

All of a sudden, the absences I'd noted earlier took on new meaning. Had our captain and alternate been disciplined for their previous behavior... or, better yet, traded?

And if so, did that mean I had a chance to become captain? Could I really be that goddamn lucky?

Fuck, I hoped so.

To my left, Jane was furiously tapping on her tablet, recording everything that was being said.

Willets cleared his throat. "I'll take questions now."

"Are our positions on the team in danger?" Brian Taylor asked.

My gut flipped over. It hadn't even occurred to me to wonder that.

Willets smiled and shook his head. "No. Everyone present for this meeting is guaranteed a place on the team for the upcoming season."

Thank God.

Nick raised his hand. "Does this mean you'll be reconsidering the team captain and alternate?"

Willets nodded. "We'll be reevaluating everything under Mr. Trent's guidance. Hopefully, our new leadership will guide the team to a brighter future."

People elbowed each other. Some whispered excitedly. I straightened, thoughts whirring through my mind.

This was it. The opportunity I'd been waiting for had just been handed to me on a golden platter.

I would not screw it up.

Willets ended the Q&A session. "Please allow me to introduce your new head coach." He gestured toward the entrance. "Coach Murray Dunn."

We all followed the movement. A tall, broad-shouldered guy with a bit of a gut and a stubbled chin straightened from where he'd been leaning against the wall beside the door. He unhooked his thumbs from his pockets and removed his ball cap.

"Hi, all." He spoke in a slow drawl, but his gaze was sharp. "You can call me Coach or Coach Dunn. I'm looking forward to getting to know you all and figuring out how we can work together to turn this team around. Before we get to it, I want you to know that I won't tolerate the same antics that your last coach did. There will be no bullying and no dirty plays. Anyone who causes problems will be dealt with."

Judging by his expression, he expected protests, but I, for one, was relieved. Our last coach had let Taggert get away with whatever he wanted. A stricter approach was just what we needed. But how could I impress him?

"We want to make this team one that knows how to win and one that has no reason to be called the loose cannons of the league. We expect your whole-hearted commitment to our goal."

Reading between the lines, he was warning us all to work hard and be on our best behavior. What would happen if anyone refused to play nice? Would they be traded too?

"There's no proper training today," he went on. "Instead, there will be a casual skate in half an hour so I can get an initial impression of where you're all at. Training camp will begin properly tomorrow. Don't be late."

My stomach dropped. So I wouldn't have the opportunity to show him my full range of skills today. Oh well. At least I'd have time to prepare for tomorrow.

Dunn and Willets left the room, leaving us to talk between ourselves.

Nick leaned toward me. "How many people are missing? Do you think they've been traded?"

"At least two." I looked around, taking a mental inventory of who'd been on the team last season but wasn't here today. A couple of players had retired, but it was still clear that several others were absent.

"Four."

We both turned to Jane, who'd dragged her chair closer and was studying her tablet, a cute little furrow between her eyebrows.

She raised her head and met our eyes. "Taggert, Halonen, Tremblay, and Olson. There are four players present who've transferred in from other teams: Gauthier, Fox, Elliot, and Schmidt—potentially to replace them because they play the same positions."

I barely resisted the urge to pump my fist. If Taggert had been kicked off the team, that was the best news I'd heard in years.

Nick looked impressed with Jane. "Are you sure you're happy staying with Heartless Harris? I could use an assistant."

She rolled her eyes. "Don't call him that. And yes, I'm happy where I am."

A flicker of warmth lit inside me. It was hardly surprising that some smart-ass had come up with that moniker, considering how hard I concentrated on hockey to the exclusion of all else—including my social life. But I only kept to myself because I'd learned early on that the people closest to me could inflict the most damage—thanks, Dad—so it felt nice to be defended.

"Are you going to call your agent?" Jane asked me.

"I suppose I'd better." He didn't like being kept in the dark. He expected to know things within seconds of them happening. Especially potentially career-altering changes such as this. "I'll be back in a minute."

I strode out into the corridor to make the call, arranging to meet with him tomorrow.

When I reentered the meeting room, Nick was chatting with Jesse, one of the younger players on the team, and Jane was still on her tablet. Sometimes I wondered if it was glued to her hand.

My agent had asked her to compile any information she had about the changes and trades, so I passed along the message, and she said she'd do it straight away. I'd known she would. I'd had assistants before her, but none as well-rounded and competent as her.

"You'd better get your gear from the car and get changed," she said, looking up briefly. "You don't want the new guys to show you up after all the hours you've put in."

She passed me the keys and I hurried down the stairs, out the side door to the parking lot to grab my duffel bag from the back seat. As I carried it inside, Jane came down the stairs and I returned the keys to her.

"Good luck," she said with a hint of a smile.

"Thanks." I hoped I didn't need it. I'd been working my ass off—not just the past few weeks, to get up to standard before the season began—but for my whole damn life.

She brushed past me and disappeared through the door. Behind me, someone sighed. I looked over at Matt, one of the defensemen, who'd been watching our exchange.

"I have no idea why in the hell someone like Jane is working for you," he said, stuffing his free hand into his pocket.

I frowned. If that was some sort of slight against Jane, we were going to have a problem.

"Matthews. Harris. Enough chitchat. Get changed," Willets barked.

We both jolted into motion, hurrying to the changing rooms and slipping inside. I made my way to my locker and paused, gazing at my name on the metal. The sight never grew old. I traced the outline of the letters, as I did every time I trained here or played a home game.

The interior of the locker was empty. I'd cleaned it out at the end of last season, but I carefully stacked everything I wouldn't need today inside, then I stripped off and changed into my gear. Clothes first, followed by tape, then skates. The order had to be right.

Five minutes later, we were on the ice.

It was a disaster.

Perhaps it was just as well that the first official training session wasn't until tomorrow. I was in good form, but it had been a while since I'd run drills with others and had a hard time getting into the flow. The rookies were either lost or trying too hard, and the guys who'd transferred didn't seem to know what to make of the rest of us.

I got it. We didn't function like other teams. We weren't a cohesive unit. We'd been in an unhealthy environment for so long that we didn't know how we were supposed to behave. It was a mindfuck.

My legs burned as I powered up the ice and intercepted a puck, internally reminding myself that I had a lot to be grateful for. There was no Taggert yelling obscenities or taking too much joy in slamming his teammates. We might be all over the place, but that toxic asshole was gone—at least temporarily— and with his departure came my opportunity.

After a couple of hours, Dunn ordered us to get our asses off the ice, shower, and be back bright and early tomorrow. I trailed behind the others, checking that nothing had been left behind. As I approached the gate, Nick came over to join me.

"Who do you think they'll make captain?" he asked.

My heart rate picked up, but I did my best to maintain a neutral expression. "Could be you."

Much as I hated to say it, he wouldn't be a bad choice. He'd played for the Chaos for five years and was one of our most well-liked players. Not that that said much since none of us got on particularly well. Our former coach had had a habit of pitting us against each other.

Nick scrunched his nose. "They'll probably want someone with a better scoring record. That could be you, if you wanted it."

I drew in a slow breath. I wanted it with everything I had, but there was no way I'd say so out loud. I was too superstitious for that.

This could be the biggest turning point of my career. If I worked my ass off, Dunn might make me captain. But this was also the last year of my contract. If he didn't like what he saw, I could lose everything.

ALSO BY A. RIVERS

Chicago Chaos Hockey

Heartless As Puck

Broken As Puck

Standalone

All Your Pucking Secrets

Crown MMA Romance

Fighter's Heart

Fighter's Best Friend

Fighter's Secret

Fighter's Second Chance

Crown MMA Romance: The Outsiders

Fighter's Frenemy

Fighter's Fake Out

Fighter's Mercy

Fighter's Forever

King's Security

The King

The Veteran

The Spy

The Liar

ABOUT THE AUTHOR

A. Rivers writes romance with strong heroes and heroines who kick butt and take names. She loves MMA fighters, private investigators, hockey players, military men, bodyguards, and the protective guy next door who isn't afraid to fight the odds for love. She also writes small town romance as Alexa Rivers.

www.ingramcontent.com/pod-product-compliance
Lightning Source LLC
Chambersburg PA
CBHW030929060726
47591CB00005B/1715